Campus answers

Check out also

**Camus Calling**
ISBN 978-1-909424-68-5


Printed by Direct-POD: April 2014

# Camus Answers

Jessie MacQuarrie

ISBN: 978- 1- 909424-71-5

Any people depicted in stock imagery provided by Thinkstock are models, and such images are being used for illustrative purposes only. Certain stock imagery © Thinkstock.

This book is printed on acid-free paper.

Because of the dynamic nature of the Internet, any web addresses or links contained in this book may have changed since publication and may no longer be valid. The views expressed in this work are solely those of the author and do not necessarily reflect the views of the publisher, and the publisher hereby disclaims any responsibility for them.

With thanks to all my friends in Scotland, particularly those on the islands of Mull and Ulva, forever my inspiration.

# REMINISCING

For Reg and Phyllis, the approach of yet another season as wardens at their beautiful caravan site was still exciting. They could hardly believe that this was to be their sixth year. Sharing their first coffee of the day, seated together on the bench outside the freshly painted reception, they reminisced for a while.

"Sometimes I just have to pinch myself" Phyllis said. "When we first applied for the position at Camus did you ever imagine it to be as wonderful as it is?"

Reg had to admit that his initial thoughts about the remoteness now seemed a distant memory. They fondly remembered the first November visit, the eternally long drive down unfamiliar, single track roads in the rapidly fading light, bringing them, at last, to Meg's welcoming B&B.

Looking across the field now bathed in sunshine the enduring beauty had become an integral part of their lives.

"Do you remember our first visit?" Reg rhetorically asked Phyllis "that lingering, shrouding sea mist. We couldn't see a thing. Just look at it now!"

It wasn't just the weather that had improved since then. Since that life-changing decision to take up the position as wardens of a caravan site, they had worked hard building up the business. Admittedly at times it had been hard. The weather hadn't always been kind and some of their guests had been challenging!

The people of the highlands had been so welcoming from the beginning. From Meg's first greeting of "Failte" to their crofting neighbours, Angus and Elaine, Reg and Phyllis had met with friendship, help and advice and after five years they both reflected and appreciated that they had now become an essential part of the community.

Reg was resourceful. His career as an Army Warrant Officer had been an excellent foundation for his role as a caravan site warden. He was still fit and strong for a man now nearly 67. He had a tremendous way with people. He was able to engage in interesting conversation, offer advice and solutions to problems but also to be assertive when required.

Phyllis was quieter in character but made up for it with her ability to indulge in endless conversation. She loved nothing better than to chat to her guests at every opportunity. Reg often retreated to his workshop once his daily duties were complete. It was here that he was able to enjoy the peace and quiet he craved and progress his plans for his latest project. He had a workshop full of expensive tools, all meticulously cleaned, with designated spaces on the extensive range of shelves. The way in which he arranged everything clearly showed his army discipline from which he had no intention to depart.

Phyllis had always enjoyed preparing and tending her hanging baskets as she had done for many years in her old Worcester bungalow. She had, by now, learnt to adjust to the colder climate at Camus and hence the slightly later season for bedding plants. Each year she prepared her baskets and troughs in Reg's workshop but often it resulted in a few cross words between them when Reg found that she had failed to clear up any spilt compost to his exacting standards. On the whole, however, they hardly argued at all. They were approaching their 40th year of marriage during which time they had learnt how to accept each other's foibles, maintaining harmony in their relationship.

"I'm going to see Elaine this morning" Phyllis told Reg "We need to finalise the website and discuss some letters she has received from the Tourist Board."

"Ok dear. I've got a few things to do while you're gone" replied Reg, in the knowledge that she would therefore be gone all morning or possibly even most of the day.

Elaine and Angus were their neighbours just along the road. They had become great friends since Reg and Phyllis had arrived at Camus. Angus was a burly Scotsman, incredibly strong and equally as resourceful as Reg. Although younger than Reg by about 15 years, the two men enjoyed each other's company and shared a similar sense of humour.

Angus called in most mornings to see how they were. He tended his croft with his sheep and highland cows and most afternoons he would venture out in his boat to check his creels. Elaine worked mainly from home using her skills in marketing which she had willingly employed in helping Reg and Phyllis with their business.

Angus and Elaine had three children. Donnie, now 19, was only 14 when Reg and Phyllis first arrived. He had been brought up on the croft and also helped his dad on the boat. Over the years they had watched him grow in to a lovely young man with a keen interest in outdoor activities including sea kayaks. Finding work locally was often a problem for the young people so when Reg, together with Angus, had decided to refurbish the boathouse Donnie, who by then was 17 and about to leave school, agreed to buy a few sea kayaks and try to encourage more, younger visitors to the site. Donnie had two siblings - a sister Paige, now eight, and a brother, Camran, ten. Angus's elderly father, Hamish, was now 87. He still owned the lease of the caravan site which was formerly part of his croft. Now a widower he lived alone in a small cottage. Angus, however, had built his own new family home which was beautiful and modern and kept impeccably by Elaine. He had done much of the construction work himself as was typical for these hardy highlanders.

It was important of course not to leave out Norman or Tormad to use his Gaelic name. He was an impressive

Highland bull and had been with Angus for almost 15 years now. He wasn't a young bull but over the years he had become more of a pet or additional member of the family; in fact he had now also become a distinctive feature of the Camus site. When Reg and Phyllis first arrived they had soon learnt how to entice him away from the quaint humped backed bridge with feed pellets. He was curious to see any new visitors and therefore regularly blocked the passage for approaching caravans. Reg and Phyllis too now looked upon him fondly, even though, at times, they had to clear up after he had wandered on to the site.

Then of course there was Meg who had been their first local contact when they arrived at her B&B. She had lived in the area all her life. Sadly she had lost her husband a few years ago and her two grown up sons had moved away. She was an endless source of local knowledge and had become a firm friend and confidant for Phyllis. Her culinary skills were exceptional and envied by Phyllis. On many occasions she had welcomed Phyllis's friends and family to her B&B when they came to visit.

Over the past five seasons Reg and Phyllis had become captivated with the area, the amazing scenery and wildlife they were regularly privileged to encounter, from the colourful birds visiting Phyllis's feeders, the pine martens seeking treats from Meg's bird table and to the occasional sightings of dolphins, minke whales and basking sharks out in the bay. Sometimes they caught a rare glimpse of their resident otter crossing the shore on its way to fish for its supper.

They had been lucky to observe the beautifully changing colours of the steep hills, sometimes lush and green, gradually changing through red, gold and brown. They had learned to observe the varied leaves of the mixture of pine and deciduous trees. Sometimes the unpredictable weather brought new surprises. A covering of sparkling frost at either end of the season added a new magical touch as if it were sprinkled by invisible fairies. Perhaps no surprise therefore that they were so lucky to have been chosen as the subject of a wildlife film last autumn. They were both really looking forward to seeing Camus on film in a matter of days and had every hope that, when shown on national TV, it would bring yet more visitors.

Looking back to when they first took on the position as wardens on behalf of Touring Haven holidays, they had not really considered for how long they might stay. They had settled in to a seasonal existence of living in their caravan at Camus from March to October and wintering back in Worcester through November to February. Their Worcester bungalow was looking increasingly tired each time they returned. It lacked the dutiful attention once paid by Reg but, it was only last year that the holiday company had announced their intention to close the site. It was true that both Reg and Phyllis now felt a real sense of belonging. Spurred on by the visit from the TV film crew and swept along by local support, they had impulsively agreed to take on an independent lease and had embarked upon their own improvements to the site. So, as the new season approached, it seemed that they were opening a new chapter for which there was no obvious ending.

Of course both Reg and Phyllis missed their family. Phyllis's elderly father Henry had sadly passed away a while back but their daughter Annie, with her husband Craig and their two children Ellie and William were still miles away in Worcester. Ryan, their son, was in the army serving in Afghanistan so they were used to not seeing him so often. They had however always enjoyed his visits the last of which was only in March when he, together with his army friend Devden had helped Reg to convert the steading.

Although they had been at Camus for five seasons, they had still been unable to visit some of the local attractions for themselves as they were normally tending to the site and their guests while the tourist season was in full swing. They had, of course, visited their friends Joyce and Jimmy who operated the Ferry Boathouse from where the regular ferry to Mull sailed and where they had had the opportunity to sample Joyce's exquisite seafood, some of which was brought ashore by Angus. Phyllis and Meg had frequently enjoyed tea and cakes at the Lighthouse and both Reg and Phyllis had made regular trips to Fort William and other places on the mainland to pick up supplies. Their guests had taken many of the trips available locally and frequently told Reg and Phyllis about their amazing experiences. Although they were fully prepared to work hard through their first independent season, Phyllis was hopeful that they might soon get the time to explore more of the area for themselves.

Reg had proudly earned the privilege to take part in the deer stalking on the local estate with Niall, the estate manager, and indeed his accurate shooting, gained through his army career, had brought him an enviable reputation even surpassing that of Angus. Since arriving at Camus Reg had lovingly restored Fergal, the old tractor long hidden in the steading, the fulfilment of a secret passion he had harboured for many years.

His recent project refurbishing the steading and turning it in to a campers retreat had just been completed, thanks to the help from his son Ryan and army friend Devden, whilst they were on leave from their unit in Afghanistan. Whilst Reg had supervised the work to ensure that it met his expected standards, he was impressed with the finished result which Donnie knew would bring in more campers and encourage more kayak trips as the new season approached. They could not take it easy however as the Tourist Board were due to inspect the site later this month and review the current 2* rating which Reg was determined to improve upon.

"I'm looking forward to meeting some of our old friends again this year" remarked Phyllis, continuing to sip her coffee. "We've got Mick and Maureen coming in May;

apparently they've got a posh new caravan; Maureen told me in her Christmas letter."

Phyllis had made it an annual event to send cards to their guests each year in the hope that it would encourage return custom.

"I can't wait to see Geoffrey and Ronnie and see what they make of my latest bird boxes" said Reg. "I've learned so much from them and their knowledge of the birds, they're really nice guys".

"The Coles are returning again but without the teenage girls, only young Max this time." announced Phyllis.

"I hope that there won't be any disasters, this time" remarked Reg "How old do you think Max is now?" I'd better warn Angus in case they take off to sea again" he laughed.

They had witnessed some memorable events over the last few years which, had passed by so quickly. Mick's obsession with cleaning his caravan, Maureen's exquisite painting of Phyllis's troughs, Geoffrey and Ronnie's photo of the barn owl leaving the steading, Angus rescuing Max and his Dad from a buoy around the headland and the sight of Mrs Shaw's huge bra, wrenched from the clothes line only to be observed floating out to sea. They would surely never forget 'Survival Man', in his camouflaged clothes, caught poaching game from Angus's croft and getting unceremoniously scared off the site by their angry, intimidating neighbour.

They had encountered many pets, mainly dogs. Reg would always remember Mr Philpott and the assistance given to the widower with his three dogs. Phyllis too was able to look back now and laugh about Houdini the Jack Russell who brought total devastation to her immaculate troughs although, at the time, she admitted to being heartbroken. Their position as wardens had allowed them to meet so many people from Britain and abroad. Most of them had been nice and a pleasure to spend time with although there were some who they hoped would not come back!

They sat together finishing their coffee and preparing to start their day. The temptation to linger and simply soak up the views never diminished but there was much work to be done.

# EVERYTHING IN
# POSITION

As Reg prised himself from the bench, the early morning April sun lit up the steading, like a series of well-positioned spotlights. It was as if new life had simply been added to the old. The fresh dawn dew had dusted the old stones with a sheen which glistened in the sunlight. Industrious spiders had been busy casting a delicate net of webbing as if they were also playing their part in holding the structure together. Tiny beads of water reflected like jewels each time that the clouds parted.

The external character of the building had remained largely unchanged. The walls still had their carefully placed stones, the embedded moss, the lichen and the evidence of habitation by tiny creatures. Reg wondered how many voles, weasels, toads, birds and insects had sought refuge in this structure since it was built. What stories would their ancestors be able to tell?

A few stones had been dislodged through the years. These were duly repositioned during the refurbishment. Reg had carefully lifted each fallen stone. In one small area he was surprised to find old, dry limpet shells clearly placed between the rocks. How could they have got there? The steading was a reasonable way from the sea. They could not have been simply discarded by a passing sea bird or else they would not have settled underneath the heavy stones. They were purposely stacked starting with a larger shell and then progressing inside with smaller and smaller ones much like a series of Russian dolls. He had not had time to research how long they had been there or why. The urgency to complete the refurbishment had forced him to put the curiosity to the back of his mind. He was determined, however, to return to the subject at some later stage so he carefully wrapped a few of the shells in some tissue for safekeeping.

Since Ryan and Devden had returned to their unit, Reg, Angus and Donnie had installed a stylish but basic kitchen in one end of the steading. There was a selection of cupboards, a simple sink and a cooker fuelled by an external gas bottle. The cupboards were made of wood, tastefully matching the long dining table which took up a large part of the room. Two benches, placed at either side, provided sufficient seating for up to eight people. Phyllis had been busy in Fort William buying the material and padding to make two long, bench cushions. Fortunately Meg had a sewing machine so Phyllis had spent many hours with her making the cushions whilst catching up on the latest gossip. She had purposely chosen a tartan cloth. Most visitors enjoyed the patterns so iconic to Scotland.

The wood burner had come from Bert, in the village. He was changing his old one and everyone knows that a Scotsman hates to see anything go to waste. A basket of logs and kindling had been placed for the first guests to use. An old sofa had also been donated by Meg's friend Morag. It was green and burgundy in colour which matched Phyllis's cushions perfectly. Donnie had painted the walls white, ensuring that as much light as possible was reflected around the room through the small, deep-set windows. Elaine had framed two photos, taken on earlier kayak trips, which Donnie had proudly hung on the walls either side of the wood burner. She had also framed the picture, taken by Geoffrey, of the barn owl leaving the steading. The barn owl had not been seen for some time but everyone was hoping that she would return now that the work to the steading was complete. Reg had made a new bird table which could be seen from the steading window. Within no time at all the feisty siskins had made it a regular feeding spot.

The first visitors were due to arrive on 2nd April. Two caravans had made a booking for the first week. No campers had yet booked but Donnie had received numerous enquiries for the Easter period. Phyllis resumed the bread orders and had stocked the shop with essential supplies. Reg made a new sign, a large board proudly announcing Camus as a caravan and camping site. Elaine had included a sketch of the steading for the use of campers and advertised the availability of kayak adventures. The sign also displayed their new telephone number. No longer would visitors be directed to Touring Haven holidays and subjected to listening to various options before selecting 1= request a brochure, 2 = make a booking, 3= cancel or change a booking.

Elaine had been in negotiation with the Scottish Tourist Board to get the typical brown signs directing people to the site and announcing the availability of kayak adventures. To secure this required Donnie to complete his BCU (British Canoe Union) coach training including Safety and Rescue. The business support offered by the Tourist Board had been very helpful. Donnie had completed the necessary courses during the winter months. The signs had been approved; however a decision regarding their placement was still needed.

From first light Reg was out positioning the bins, followed by his daily inspection of the site making sure that everything was in order. Should he spot anything even slightly out of position he would be sure to correct it. Norman had sneaked onto the site and had left a large deposit right in the middle of the tarmac entrance. Reg was not impressed and quickly got his spade, a broom and a bucket of water from the shed.

"Well that's not a very nice welcome for our first guests" Reg advised Norman. "They won't want to be treading that in to their caravans will they? Why don't you go down to the bridge to wait for them" he continued, giving him a firm pat on the backside to move him on.

For each of the previous seasons, Reg had felt obliged to follow the wardens' instruction manual supplied by Touring Haven holidays. This included a schedule of tasks, be they daily, weekly or seasonal. Some were obvious like emptying the bins but some were weekly or periodic, such as cleaning out the drains. Over the winter, Reg had compiled his own manual. He had also paid particular attention to Health and Safety ensuring that the stringent requirements of the Tourist Board were met. Under the management of Touring Haven Holidays the site had been awarded a 2* rating. True to form, Reg was determined to improve that at least to 3*, even aiming towards 4*.

Now that the steading was finished, he had arranged for a representative from the tourist board to visit after Easter to review the current rating. The facilities of the steading would be sure to impress: somewhere to cook, eat, wash-up and even dry clothes. He had spent a lot of time on the internet comparing Camus with other sites. He knew that Camus currently offered no dedicated disabled facilities in the washrooms, an issue he was fully prepared to address.

Phyllis had learnt from the past few years that her display of bedding plants would not be ready until June, therefore before they left Camus at the end of last season they had planted the troughs with beautiful spring bulbs. The crocuses, tulips and daffodils were now adding wonderful colour around the reception. Phyllis was very happy with the result.

Reg was delighted to see that once again his bird boxes were in use. He had added a new larger box, having checked the size on the internet. He had hoped to attract some of the woodpeckers he had seen around the site. He had picked a tree on the edge of the site and fixed the box higher than usual. From the tell-tale sign of wood chippings, found at the base of the tree, he felt sure that it was in use although he had yet to see any birds entering or leaving. Other boxes were certainly occupied by tenants - possibly blue tits, great tits or maybe coal tits. Reg had deliberately placed the woodpecker nest box far away from the boxes which were for the smaller birds, aware that, although lovely to watch, the woodpeckers were not averse to drilling larger holes in order to steal the chicks nurtured by the tits. He had therefore secured a neat metal surround protecting the openings of the smaller boxes. In the past he had caught sight of both the greater spotted and also the green woodpeckers. Phyllis had seen them too, taking peanuts from her feeders.

Reg wished that he had the camera equipment and the knowledge that the wildlife crew had brought with them last season. They had kindly agreed to show an early screening in the school hall just before the Easter holidays. Camran and Paige were so excited. They felt like they were about to attend a premier.

"Phyllis, do you think that I will be in the film?" asked Paige.

"I'm not sure dear" replied Phyllis "Maybe, but I think that the men were actually looking at the animals."

"My friends at school are looking forward to it" Paige continued. "Rosie and Kyle think that I'm going to be a star!"

"My teacher said that we should have a class visit to see all the bird boxes and the bird tables" added Camran. "Do you think that we could all come Reg?"

"Of course you can" replied Reg "I'll have to pick a day when we're not too busy though."

Reg and Phyllis had received updates from the film company regarding their forthcoming visit to the school. It would be on the 5th April just before the Easter school holidays. Elaine had drafted a letter to the parents to invite them and many had replied regarding their intention to attend. As it was only a small school of 30 children and the assembly hall would, at most, accommodate a maximum of 40 small chairs, it was therefore arranged that there would be a viewing for the smaller children and parents at 2pm and another at 4pm for the older children and guests. Some dignitaries were also invited, including the local Minister. This was to be a major event in the village and surrounding area. Everybody was talking about it and Phyllis was hoping that bookings for the season would come flooding in after its showing on national TV over the Easter Bank Holiday. She had thoughtfully invited a representative from the Tourist Board to come to the later screening in recognition of the help they had given producing posters for display both in their own offices and in local shops, pubs and community halls. Everything was going so well and even Reg showed an uncharacteristic excitement amidst his normally serious and focused demeanour.

It was Saturday the 2nd April and the first caravans were due to arrive that afternoon - a Mr and Mrs Willis from the Midlands who had not been before but who had booked for three weeks, much longer than Camus usual guests. The other pre-booked guests were a couple from the West Country. They were in for a long journey but Reg expected that they had almost certainly stopped en route. It was therefore difficult to predict at what time they might arrive.

When the Willis's arrived they had an older, large caravan which was obviously well-loaded. Mr Willis was a larger than life, cheerful guy and his wife similarly was warm and bubbly. They pulled onto the site and met Phyllis in the reception. Once in Phyllis's grasp it was usual for guests to stay and chat for ages. There was a lot to report about the journey, the long stretch from the ferry, the time it had taken, the humped back bridge and - frequently - Norman. However Norman had obviously been caught unawares. He wasn't smart enough to anticipate the start of the new season and was therefore not tuned in yet to the arrival of new guests. Reg waited outside in case the Willis's needed help pitching up. He was pacing around wondering how much longer Phyllis would keep them talking. Eventually they emerged but as they were the first van on site they had the choice of any pitch. Reg asked if he could be of any help but Mrs Willis politely declined, saying that they were 'old hands' at this game.

Predictably they chose a front pitch and Mr Willis reversed the van, leaving sufficient space for his awning.

Caravanners will, no doubt, be aware that when setting up on site every move is watched intently by others. Phyllis had still retained the urge to study from the reception. Mr Willis had a full-size awning and an extension for the dog. He erected the awning quite quickly and then started to unload both the car and the contents of the caravan.

"Just come and look at this Reg" whispered Phyllis as Reg passed by.

"What is it?" asked Reg.

"I've never seen guests with so much stuff" she said.

"I thought that the van looked a bit heavy" he said. At this point Reg felt equally compelled to watch from the window. He did not normally indulge in this frivolous pastime but, on this occasion, he found himself absorbed.

First there was a large ground sheet covering the entire floor of the awning. Next came two folding dining chairs and a table which had been stacked in the back of the estate car. This was followed by two sun loungers and a coffee table stored in the caravan hold. Then two further folding tables were allocated a place around the edge of the awning. Why on earth were so there so many tables?

"I fancy a cup of tea. Would you like me to make you one dear?" asked Reg. There was a limit to how much time he could spend being a casual observer.

The unpacking continued. Phyllis used her binoculars, hiding partially behind the decorative curtain. She was having trouble making out all the objects which were appearing in succession. Because the Willis's had chosen a pitch right at the front of the site they had made this quite difficult for her. She could now, however, make out a halogen heater, a series of extension leads, an electric griddle or grill, a microwave, a portable music centre and a wok. From the caravan itself they brought out a huge dog bed, rather oversized for their Pomeranian pet, and a selection of dog bowls and toys. These were placed in the awning extension. As if this were not enough, they had also brought with them a number of wind chimes, bright plastic wind spinners and coloured garden candle holders. Setting up all this paraphernalia was taking a considerable time. No wonder they had planned for such a long stay.

Reg had moved back outside. Angus's pick up pulled onto the site for his daily catch up. Immediately Angus could see that Reg was a bit grumpy.

"Look at those ornaments all flapping in the wind" he grunted at Angus "Looks like a stall at a fair ground!"

Angus laughed "A bit different" he admitted. "They've obviously collected them on their travels but I wouldn't spend money on that load of tat" he added, not holding back in expressing his opinion.

At the moment the wind was light but the two men wondered how long the decorations would stay in place once the breeze picked up and the wind chimes did exactly what they were designed to do.

By mid afternoon the couple from the West Country arrived. They pulled up to the reception followed by Norman but they seemed reluctant to get out of their car until Reg came out and shooed him away. They stepped inside to complete Phyllis's forms and sign in.

"Welcome" said Phyllis "You must be Mr and Mrs Vessey. Have you had a good journey?"

"Yes" replied Mr Vessey "We stopped at Carlisle last night and just did this last stretch today."

"It's beautiful here, isn't it" added Mrs Vessey "I can't wait to look around".

It was a particularly lovely day and the site with its views was at its best.

"We've only got one other van at the moment but then, today, is the first day of the season. We are expecting more to arrive though." Phyllis advised. "Would you like to choose your pitch and then come back so that I can give you a tour of the site and the facilities?"

Mrs Vessey said that she would which pleased Phyllis who loved to mix the tour with the customary chat. She thought that she might offer to take both the Vessey's and the Willis's around together. Reg had, however, beaten her to it and could be seen escorting Mr and Mrs Willis around the site. Reg had introduced himself and in turn found out that their names were Margaret and Tony. He was clearly so proud of the steading that he couldn't wait to show them. Although it had been designed particularly for campers he wanted to assure them that they too could use it although they had obviously come so well equipped he doubted that it would offer anything not already contained in their awning.

"You've done a grand job with this" complimented Tony.

"I love the cushions" added Margaret "It will be so cosy in here for the campers especially when it's cold and wet".

"Have you been to this area before?" asked Reg.

"No, we've been to Scotland every year but not to this part. We've been to Fort William and to Skye but we've never ventured across the Corran ferry. I've recently had a heart by-pass so we looked for somewhere quieter this year" replied Tony.

"Well it's certainly peaceful here" added Reg "There's a load to do though. You must go and see Phyllis. She has lots of leaflets in the reception of boat trips, wildlife, places to go, restaurants etc".

Phyllis was still watching the Vesseys set up on their pitch. She was itching to give them a tour but they appeared to be taking their time. They had a small porch awning which they erected quite quickly but Phyllis could clearly see that they were preparing a cup of tea so it would be rude to go now. It was an hour later before she felt compelled to interrupt.

"Hello again" she called from outside the awning "are you ready for me to show you the facilities?"

"Yes please, just give us a minute" said Mrs Vessey.

"As I said my name is Phyllis and my husband is Reg. We have been the wardens here for five years but now we run the site ourselves".

"I'm Barbara and this is Tom" she replied.

"Oh I used the love 'The Good Life'" said Phyllis laughing to her self. "I suppose that everyone says that to you."

"Yes we've heard it a few times before" said Tom.

Phyllis couldn't exactly tell from his tone whether he had shared the joke or been irritated by it so she quickly moved them on to the shoreline. As well as the superb views she pointed out the boathouse and the kayaks arranged neatly outside. She told them about Donnie and his business and soon found that she was also telling them about Angus and his boat and Elaine who had given her so much help with the web-site. She took them to the washrooms and was pleased to see that they looked suitably impressed. Phyllis led them to the steading, telling them about how she and Reg had converted it only a few weeks ago and how their son

Ryan had returned from Afghanistan to help out. She was so proud of him having given up all his leave. She started to tell Tom and Barbara about the old tools they had found in the steading but as Tom was already returning outside Phyllis quickly followed. Her next subject was the visit last year from the film crew. She was so looking forward to seeing the film in the school next week. The Vessey's were both tired however, having had a long journey, and seemed anxious to return to their van. Phyllis could sense that the tour was over and reluctantly agreed to let them stroll round later when they were up to it.

"Do come and see me in the reception" she said as she walked away. "I've got lots of information that you will find useful."

No unexpected guests arrived that day so when Reg and Phyllis retired to their caravan for the evening they both felt relaxed and happy.

"I think that we should have a little drink with our dinner" suggested Reg. "What do you think dear?"

"Yes please" replied Phyllis "I'll have a small glass of wine. I think that the first day of the new season has started well. I've got a good feeling about this year".

# CAMUS WATCH

As the week progressed Phyllis received yet more bookings. Some were referrals from the Tourist Information Centre and several were bookings made following a visit to their own website. They were all reservations for Easter, so the season was off to a good start.

On the Tuesday 5th April everyone was looking forward to the film in the school hall. Phyllis heard the locals refer to it as 'Camus Watch the premier' and she asked whether herself and Reg could attend separate performances so that one of them would be on the site at all times. Reg would go to the earlier performance with Meg and Niall and Phyllis would go, with Camran and Paige, to the later one. The film was due to be shown on the BBC on Saturday 16th April. The Tourist Board were preparing a leaflet based on the film and Camus was expecting to receive a flood of bookings as a result.

The excitement in the school hall was reaching fever pitch with children giggling as their parents arrived. Reg was treated as a celebrity as he took his allotted seat. He had been asked to make an introductory speech to the audience and had spent the last few days choosing his words carefully so as to appeal to both young and old. He stood up at the front with great pride, took a deep breath and started....

"You all know by now that my wife, Phyllis, and I manage the caravan site just down the road. We've been here for five years now and we just love it. You've all made us feel so welcome. We love the scenery and the wildlife but do you know what children? We didn't realise what the animals get up to when we're not looking. Do you want to find out?"

Following squeals of "Yes, yes, yes" from the children Reg continued....

"Well last autumn we were lucky to be chosen as the subject of a wildlife film. It's going to be shown on the TV over the Easter holidays. Look carefully and you might recognise some of the animals". He was of course referring to Tormad. "I hope that you enjoy it so get comfy, sit quietly and watch."

The film started, of course, with Tormad, standing proudly on the bridge, poking out his tongue, resulting in both laughter and rapturous applause from the audience. This was followed by a sequence of birds who were regular visitors to Phyllis's feeders. The camera work was so clever. Most striking was the bright yellow of the siskins. The territorial defence of their chosen perch was often violent but effective. They are a lively member of the finch family and, although smaller than the great tits and the chaffinches, they certainly proved an ability to stand their ground. Reg admired this greatly. The male birds have a distinct black cap and bib whilst the females have more streaks on their bellies.

The siskins were however frequently interrupted by an intruding red squirrel. It scaled the feeder masterfully. The small but powerful claws hung on with determination. Once a peanut had been extracted, he or she would hastily run off up the nearest tree and sit calmly in the branch, nibbling away. The film captured the chestnut colouring, the classic white tummy, the pointed, furry ears and the curved bushy tail. Phyllis loved the way that the tail hugged the squirrel's spine. It was as if it was proudly sporting an expensive fur coat. It was lovely to see in such detail with the use of close-up footage. At the time of filming the squirrel had started to grow the longer winter coat including the larger, cute ear tufts. According to the presenter, mating would be expected during either February or March meaning that kittens would be born perhaps in April or even into May, so unfortunately there was no footage of the babies. They would not be able to be seen until much later in the year.

The crew had captured a cute bank vole scurrying around near the burn. It would appear hurriedly but cautiously stop occasionally, when it found something tasty to eat. In one scene it could be seen eating a worm, in another it appeared to have found some kind of root from deep within the vegetation. Having found some food, it would scurry back into the undergrowth. Being that the creature was so small, it took considerable effort to lift and drag the heavy root back to the safety of cover. The presenter revealed that, in the autumn, bank voles sometimes store food in preparation for the forthcoming winter. Phyllis recognised the voice of Matt. He had a lovely way of describing this miniature safari captured on camera. The children obviously found the scene amusing, giggling as the vole frequently dropped the food and was forced to return to retrieve its prize.

The film lasted 40 minutes. Reg and Phyllis now saw the animals as never before. They both felt that from listening to Matt they had learnt a lot and from now on they would surely watch for all the tell-tale signs, such as distinctive footprints or droppings revealing the animal's diet. At the later showing, Phyllis noted that the children squirmed at the mention of 'poo' and even she thought that actually picking up and smelling it was a little unnecessary! They felt that once the film was shown on national TV it would attract considerable attention. Meg was also hopeful that the amazing pictures of the pine martens visiting her bird table would also bring new B&B guests. The film certainly was the point of discussion for all the locals. There was footage of Angus's creels and of the deer on Niall's estate. The local shop was full of enthusiasm and had already added a selection of furry toys to the gift counter. The pocket-sized RSPB bird book was now on sale and the selection of postcards was increased to include yet more pictures of the local wildlife.

Whilst Reg and Phyllis revelled in the attention that the screening brought they were concerned that visitors might, in future, assume that wildlife sightings were guaranteed when in reality they were not. This gave Reg food for thought.

By Wednesday the wind had picked up considerably. The Willis's display of wind chimes and spinners was in full action. Together they resulted in a cacophony of noise, not exactly in keeping with Camus's usual serenity. Margaret and Tony Willis seemed oblivious but Reg was hopeful that they would soon get fed up and take down the hideous ornaments. Mr Willis came to the conclusion that the awning would soon be blow down in the strong Atlantic onslaught. He came to the reception to ask Reg where he could get some storm straps to make sure that his awning was doubly secure. Phyllis directed him to Fort William, some distance away. Tony asked whether Reg would like him to get a few more for his stock in case any other guests would like some. Reg declined politely. He was now in his 6th season and, although he had experienced many a flapping awning, it was usually because it had not been properly secured to the ground. Considering though, the vast contents of the Willis's awning, Reg was quite happy for him to take whatever precautions he felt necessary.

The Vesseys too had by now been on site for a few days. They had been to the reception several times, taking away a selection of brochures. As it was Wednesday they had booked the trip to the Treshnish Isles especially to see the puffins, first taking Jimmy's ferry to Mull. Phyllis remembered her newlywed guests Chris and Melanie and their memorable trip. Since then it had become quite a favourite with so many visitors and Phyllis was becoming increasingly jealous. She would love to go herself but always seemed to be too busy.

General polite conversation invariably revealed each guest's occupation, either current or previous. Mr Willis used to do loft conversions and had his own business and Mrs Willis was a midwife. When Phyllis found out, that opened up a whole new topic of conversation.

"Oh I had a terrible time with Annie, my eldest," she gasped "I swore at the time that I would never have another but I did. I've got a son Ryan; he is in the army in Afghanistan."

"If I had a penny for every time I've heard a new mum saying 'there won't be anymore' I'd be a rich woman" laughed Margaret.

Although Phyllis had made a tenuous link to Margaret's occupation she felt compelled to tell her that they were expecting more babies this spring - Norman was going to be a dad again. Margaret had, of course, been introduced to Norman as he had blocked the bridge when they went to the town on Monday. Norman had been the proud father to calves many times before and, this year Angus had three cows, all expecting Norman's babies!

Margaret seemed relatively uninterested but Phyllis was quite proud. She now looked upon Norman with an affection normally reserved for pets. The calves were expected from April onwards. Angus had been breeding on a small scale for several years and regularly went to the cattle market in Oban to get Norman some new lady friends.

Inspired by the TV film, Reg busied himself in his workshop making a large A-frame blackboard to position just outside reception. This was to be used by visitors to report wildlife sightings. Reg had painted lines which separated the board into designated slots. He had also painted fixed headings of Date? Time? Where? Animal? He fixed a Tupperware container to the board to hold chalks and a sponge. Phyllis complimented this by dedicating a more permanent 'wildlife diary' in the reception where either she or the guests themselves could record their sightings. They looked forward to the season ahead and the entries that would be made.

The Willis's duly headed for Fort William and Tony returned sporting the storm straps he had deemed necessary to add to the awning. With Reg's help they soon had the straps secured to the ground and spread them across the awning roof. Tony was content with this latest addition and felt that he could now relax for the duration.

After a few days other vans would arrive and the first campers were expected by the weekend. The wind had died down considerably, rendering Mr Willis's storm straps yet another unnecessary addition to his endless equipment. The forecast for the Easter period was good, giving everyone the opportunity to see Camus at its best.

Mr and Mrs Vessey were off for the day. They took the boat trip to Mull and crossed the island by minibus to the Ulva Ferry, from where they would get another boat, the 'Hoy Lass', operated by Turus Mara, to go to the Treshnish islands. The skipper, Iain, had a great sense of humour and gave a wonderful commentary as the boat left the Ulva Ferry pier. He started by welcoming them all on board using a greeting in Gaelic but quickly laughed as he told them 'that was enough of that silly language'!

On the way out they headed west, around the shore of Ulva through Loch Na Keal. He directed their attention first to an uninhabited island 'Eorsa' which, he was proud to announce, was famous for 'absolutely nothing'. Mrs Vessey found this really funny. In the distance he pointed out the location of Ormaig, a deserted township once the seat of the MacQuarrie clan. It was not possible to see the cluster of derelict buildings even through their binoculars but the skipper said that there were many walks on Ulva, one of which took you to this now silent village. Just past Ormaig were a series of tiny outcrops of land which, the skipper advised, were referred to as 'skerries'. The term 'skerry' is derived from the Old Norse (sker) which means a rock in the sea. It is used to define a small rocky island too small for habitation. In the peppermint blue waters lit up by the overhead sun, these skerries appeared surreal and tempting but the boat sped on, with Iain pointing out the basalt rock cliff edges of Ulva which would soon be surpassed by those at their next destination, the isle of Staffa.

It took a good hour to get to Staffa, passing Little Colonsay and the shores of Gometra. As they eventually came nearer to Staffa, Iain told them that the name Staffa once again comes from Old Norse for stave or pillar island. Barbara had seen pictures of the island on a leaflet, giving details of the boat trip, but as their small vessel came closer it was the size and expanse of the basalt pillars up against the boat that impressed her. They seemed unreal and were entirely formed from volcanic activity. The whole island looked like it was tilting, starting with a layer of tuff or volcanic ash, topped by towering colonnades, a colourful mixture of black and grey forming the walls and the caves of much of the island. These columns were the result of a slow cooling of the lava whereas the layer above, although equally of volcanic construction, lacked the same structure as the columns below and appeared more like a mismatched topping.

Eventually the boat swung round and the famous cavernous mouth of Fingal's Cave came into view. Unfortunately their boat was not allowed to enter the cave itself but was able to get close enough for those on board to look inside. At that moment the skipper played a pre-recording of Felix Mendelssohn's Hebrides Overture for which the island is famous. Everyone on the boat laughed and joined in the well known tune with either a hum or a poor version of la-la-la.

Iain gave them another snippet of information, telling his passengers that the cave itself is also known as An Uamh Binn (Cave of Melody) and that it has a unique, cathedral-like structure made from hexagonal columns.

The boat moored up to a man-made landing stage from where it was possible to step gingerly around the exposed basalt to enter the cave itself, aided by a thick metal rope secured in to the rock. Equally precarious was a steep set of stairs taking visitors to the lush green island top. The skipper said that a walk to the far side might well result in the first sight of puffins but it was not necessary as on the next island, Lunga, wall-to-wall puffins were assured. Based on this advice, Tom and Barbara decided to sit in the soft grass above, break out the lunch and take in the glorious views. Looking down to the sea below they were drawn by the basalt outcrops curving up from the sea softened only by outcrops of pink thrift, whilst around their immediate picnic site they could see delicate violet-blue flowers just starting to open. There was no longer any livestock on the island and therefore no grazing, leaving the natural beauty unspoilt throughout the year.

Staffa held a certain mystique but soon it was time to return to the boat and head towards Lunga. As they came closer to Lunga, they could see puffins on the surface of the sea congregating in rafts with several flying across the boat and heading for the cliff edges. The excitement on the boat was noticeably building, especially when one with outstretched wings and bright orange feet went right over Iain's cabin on its way to the shore. On Lunga, unlike Staffa, there was no purpose-made landing stage and the process involved the crew in securing a floating jetty to the boat and towing it the 100 metres or so to the island. The passengers were then helped ashore across the rocks, finally reaching a reasonable climb towards the cliff tops. The puffins were arriving in large numbers, seeking out suitable places for nesting and to await the return of their mate. Tom and Barbara found a spot in the grass and quickly sat down to get their cameras ready. They were fairly close to a burrow which was already occupied, judging by the curious sound below. Wall-to-wall puffins were no exaggeration as they came flying in from all angles, some arriving in a seeming state of panic before staggering over to find their nest. There was considerable squabbling and scrapping between them. Barbara felt that she could simply stay and watch these comical characters for hours. She could even see puffins happily occupying burrows right alongside their rabbit neighbours.

The wind had passed and the sea was quite calm. Barbara was amazed at how close she was able to get to the puffins. Sadly there were no chicks or 'pufflings' yet, they would not be visible until at least July, but the whole cliff top was a hive of activity. There were constant comings and goings by the parents, swapping over the important responsibility of incubation whilst the other returned to sea to fish. Apparently the puffins on Lunga are quite happy to welcome the human visitors as it keeps other predators such as skewers and black backed gulls away. Perhaps that explains why they are so willing to pose for endless camera shots.

Tom and Barbara had certainly enjoyed their wonderful trip and, upon their return to Camus, they proudly showed Phyllis the pictures on their camera. By now she had seen similar photos taken by many guests but still loved to see more and hear their stories. Barbara had even captured the iconic image of a puffin with a beak full of sand eels. The bird had probably dutifully brought the catch back for its mate busy incubating the egg back in the burrow.

"I really must get a day off so that I can go and see them for myself" Phyllis sighed.

"Haven't you been yet?" asked a surprised Barbara.

"No" replied Phyllis. "The trip including Jimmy's ferry takes all day and we have to be here looking after the guests. One day I will go there though."

They proceeded to be the first entry on both Reg's board and Phyllis's diary, taking great care to write neatly and make sure that they gave an outstanding review of Turus Mara which would be sure to encourage others to take the same trip.

By the end of the week Donnie was giving the final, welcoming touches to the steading. Elaine had been out collecting a few spring flowers and grasses which she placed in a vase on the table. Phyllis had placed a small amount of washing up liquid, by the sink and had pinned a notice both by the sink and washing machine to say that washing tablets and washing up liquid could be purchased from the reception. A few old magazines together with yet more leaflets showing places to visit were also left on the table for campers to read.

The first campers were a group of students from Loughborough University. Being sporty they had been attracted by the kayak trips and of course the walking. They came with three dome tents, sufficient for all six, - two girls and four strapping young men. They chose a space not too far from the steading and although they had seen the images on the website they were obviously impressed as Donnie showed them around. They were seasonal campers but they had not found many sites with such great facilities.

The two girls, Carly and Megan, were both 20 and in the second year of their degrees. Carly was studying English and Sports Science and Megan was part way through Economics with Accounting. Donnie was slightly younger being only 19 but although he had not been to university himself, he was clever and articulate and felt comfortable in the company of others who shared his passion for the outdoors. The four boys were all eager to book some kayak trips. One, called Tom, was particularly muscular and it emerged that he was a key figure in the Uni. rowing team, keen to extend his skills to kayaks.

Their tents went up without a hitch so, together with Donnie; they retired to the steading to break out some beers. Meg had kindly made some drop scones which were well received. She told Donnie that this would not be a regular treat but that it was nice as a welcome for his first visitors.

In an attempt to prevent Norman from repeating his performance in the middle of the tarmac, Reg had made a new signs and fixed them to both sides of the old barred entrance gate so that they could be seen whether entering or leaving the site.

We ask that you please close the gate behind you. Thank you.

Now that more campers were expected it would not be desirable for Norman to mess the grass. Reg had spent ages before the season started repairing the areas devastated during the winter by wild deer coming down from the hills to the site in search of richer pasture. The tent area with its layer of thick grass was a definite draw. The deer would scrape the ground clearing away any snow or frost in order to get to the juicy shoots below. Reg had tidied up the grass well and, since then, he ensured that the gate remained shut, determined to keep the site in a good state of repair.

Norman was used to spending time around the steading but those days were now over although he could often be found near the gate awaiting any opportunity to sneak back. Having gone to the bridge to give any new visitors the once-over, he loved nothing more than to follow the unsuspecting caravans back to the site. Many an unwary arrival stepping out of their vehicle to gain access to Camus would quickly step back into their car at the sight of those pointed horns thus leaving Norman free to roam until Reg or Phyllis would shoo him away.

The students were keen to explore the area. They told Donnie that they planned to embark upon a few kayak trips during the following week. The boys were hoping to make it across the Sound to the distant islands. The girls were particularly looking forward to seeing some wildlife, especially an otter. Donnie said that they would all have to start with a Health and Safety briefing in the steading the following morning. He explained that he would then spend the rest of the morning assessing their abilities before he could suggest some suitable trips. Donnie made sure that he asked them how they knew about the kayaking from the site.

"Our friends came here camping last summer" revealed James "they posted some awesome pictures on Facebook!"

"They're all talking about it at Uni" added Mark "I think that several more are planning to come during the summer".

"I've been looking after the 'freshers' this year" Paul laughed "They're all up for it but then they're up for anything"

The joke went down well and resulted in the group telling Donnie loads of funny stories about the antics of the first year students. Donnie was really pleased to hear that the word was passing round just as he had hoped. His deal, struck with the students at the start of his venture, seemed to have worked. The news and photos on Facebook were the best free publicity.

"Would you like to come and see the kayaks?" asked Donnie

They didn't need to be asked twice. Complete with beer in their hands, the students raced down to the shore to check out the kayaks. In his typically mad determination to get there first, one of the boys, Paul, tried to bound across the rocks rather than sensibly descend the slipway and, having slipped on a kelp-covered stone, went hurtling forwards, landing in a heap on the shore, gashing his knee and his nose at the same time!

The boys were all well-built, fit and with an obvious display of muscles. Donnie was panic stricken at the sight of blood pouring from Paul's injuries but the others collapsed in hysterics as Paul picked himself up without any apparent concern for his wounds.

"It had to be you!" laughed Tom "one beer and you just can't be trusted."

Donnie was going to get the first aid kit from Reg although the others assured him that it was not necessary.

"He's had worse than that most weeks on the rugby pitch" revealed James "broken limbs, smashed nose. That's only a scratch!"

" Yeah but I usually give as good as I get" added Paul "do you remember that no. 8 who I knocked out stone cold?"

"You're really living up to the reputation of being a 'Woozie Ozzie'" said Tom with obvious reference to the fact that Paul had previously earned that accolade.

"I'll still go and get something. After all we don't want to get blood on the kayaks do we?" said Donnie quickly picking up on the butch reaction of his guests. He now assumed that Paul came from Australia. He thought that he had detected an accent but he had not, until now, been able to place it. He soon returned with a large bandage and some plasters to cover Paul's knee.

Once he was patched up they all went to the boathouse to see the kayaks. There were several different types: kayaks with two seats, a number of single person sea kayaks and a few old kayaks which Donnie kept for training. He had eight in total plus his own which was his pride and joy. It stood out as the best and was clearly aimed at the best and most experienced kayaker.

While Donnie was busy with the group there was real excitement in the reception. A young couple arrived with an immaculate but very old retro caravan. It dated back to the 1980's, a Cotswold Windrush 2 berth which had been fully restored with a beautiful interior. It reminded Phyllis of her first van and she was delighted when Sarah checked in and asked her to come and look round when they got settled. They were a couple in their 30's and filled in the visitor book as Mr and Mrs Mills or Sarah and Andy as they preferred to be called.

They chose a pitch overlooking the sea drawn by the spectacular views. Little did they anticipate when they pitched up the colourful sunsets they were destined to observe. They positioned their van with the front window looking out to sea, right next to the Willis's but fortunately not obscured by their neighbour's substantial awning. Sarah and Andy did not have an awning which would have detracted from their lovingly restored van. As soon as they had sorted out the water, the waste and the hook-up, Sarah returned to the reception to invite Phyllis for a cup of tea. Phyllis had been watching from her window and could hardly wait.

As they crossed the site, Phyllis could see that the van had the old fashioned A-frame without the modern Alco stabiliser system. It looked in excellent condition with one large window to the front and one at each side. There was a door towards the back and another smaller window to the rear. Arriving at the van, Phyllis carefully stepped inside to the kitchen area at the back. She was immediately impressed by the pretty floral curtains, which were white with bright red poppies. The fabric covering the cushions was new and striped and there was a selection of retro utensils hanging proudly in the kitchen. They even had a bright red retro kettle on the gas hob.

As with Phyllis's old vans, there was no fixed bed. The two front seats simply made into a double bed each night. Phyllis remembered those times and how making the bed at the end of each day was part of their holiday. Packing the cushions tightly so that they were still in the same place come the morning was a fine art. Phyllis, being older, now appreciated the comfort of a fixed bed but she had such lovely memories of their old vans and it was great to see a young couple still enjoying those pleasures.

Whilst sharing their tea' Andy told Phyllis that he was hoping to try some sea fishing during their stay. He had recently taken up the hobby but wasn't very good at it yet.

"You must meet our neighbour Angus" Phyllis said "He has his own boat and I know that he goes fishing with his sons. I think that he sometimes takes other people. I could always ask him if you want me to."

"Yes please" Andy replied "I haven't had a chance to look around yet. Are there any other places where you can hire boats?"

"Not that I know of" Phyllis responded. "The waters round here are no place for novices. I suppose that you've seen the signs for Donnie's kayaks. Donnie is Angus's eldest son and he runs a business from here down by the old boathouse but I don't think it's suitable for fishing. If you come into the reception I have loads of leaflets telling you all about the area, places to visit, wildlife to see etc."

"I'm not too good with the water" Sarah revealed sheepishly "I can't swim very well but I'm happy for Andy to go without me. I love to read so I'm quite happy to stay here with a good book".

Phyllis looked round and saw that there was obviously no sign of a TV. "Camus is going to be on the tele soon" she announced. "We had a TV crew here last autumn and they made a lovely programme of the wildlife on the site. We saw it at the school last Tuesday and it was amazing. I'll have to speak to Reg about getting a TV set up in the steading so that people can watch it if they want."

Phyllis had finished her tea but went on to tell them all about the steading and what Reg, together with her son Ryan, had done. She offered to give them a tour but they politely declined and said that they would walk around themselves a little later. As Sarah collected the mugs, Phyllis realised that she should leave them to it so she left to find

Reg and tell him all about her idea of setting up a TV in the steading.

Of course Phyllis had put up one of the posters prepared by the Tourist Board for the TV screening. The student campers wanted to see it and, as they would be staying for 10 days, it meant that they would still be at Camus on 16th when it was due to be shown. Coincidentally they stopped Phyllis en route across the site to ask where they might be able to watch it.

"Does the film feature the otters?" asked Megan.

"Yes, it does" Phyllis replied.

"Oh I really want to watch it" said an excited Carly.

"Well I'm just on my way to find Reg" informed Phyllis "follow me. He won't be able to turn down three women" she laughed.

Reg was busy in his workshop. He was cleaning the guns that he used for clay pigeon shooting. When he was asked about a TV his first reaction was where would he get a TV, but he knew that if he were to ask around there might well be a spare one somewhere in the village. There was only a week to go so it was yet another job to squeeze on to his carefully prepared list. He was cross that he had not thought of it before but then most caravans now have their own televisions and he had left the needs of the campers for Donnie to sort out.

The following morning Reg went to see Donnie who had also been approached by the two girls and, being charmed by their pleas, had agreed to bring the large flat screen TV from his room at home. As to whether a TV would be a permanent addition to the steading was questionable. Donnie was hopeful that they would spend more time outside and had plans to organise evening kayak trips, BBQs etc. Over the next few days he made suitable arrangements for the TV and the aerial connection to be in place.

# MESSING ABOUT
# ON THE WATER

For Donnie, the schedule for the Saturday started with a health and safety briefing for the students. They gathered around the table in the steading and Donnie handed out pre-printed sheets, requiring them to read and then sign, indicating that they had understood the content. Part of the form asked about existing medical conditions. There was a great deal of banter directed at Paul. Did the Woozie Ozzie need to declare his latest injuries? Donnie laughed and replied that it wasn't necessary. He then took them down to the boathouse to be fitted with suitable wet suits, shoes and life jackets and listen to further briefings relating to the equipment and its use.

Putting on the wetsuits was a humorous affair. Donnie had bought a range of sizes but he only had two suitable for XL which were quickly snapped up by Tom and James. That left Paul and Mark to try to squeeze themselves in to two rather undersized 'large' suits struggling to pull up the zips. They tried walking somewhat awkwardly avoiding any damage to their delicate parts and retracting their muscles in to any available space. They strapped on the lifejackets and each, in turn, tested the whistle strapped neatly to the buoyancy aid.

Donnie now had to choose the most suitable kayaks from his complement of eight. The girls only wanted to venture around the coast in the hope of seeing otters but the boys wanted more excitement. To be safe Donnie decided that he would take the boys, just two at a time, for a short induction and assessment, taking the individual sea kayaks. The craft for the girls would be sorted out later.

"I'll take the boys out across the bay, two at a time, and then this evening I'll do a special trip for the girls" announced Donnie. "The evening is best for the otters as they tend to come out as dusk falls".

They carried the kayaks across the shore to the water's edge, this time, treading carefully over the rugged but slippery stones and taking great care to step over the long strips of shiny brown kelp which littered the shoreline. Getting into the kayaks was amusing. The boys, who were all fit and able, seemed to make quite a meal of it apart from Tom with his Uni rowing expertise. The other three - Mark, James and Paul - struggled to get the feel of the kayak and looked for a short while as if they were about to tip over, made worse by the splashing and boyish attempts to upturn each other. Donnie was close at hand and fairly soon he joined in the riot of laughter. Paul seemed to be the butt of many of the jokes but he was used to it and took no offence. As planned, Donnie took them in pairs across the bay. First was James and Paul then it was the turn of Mark and Tom. The girls watched from the shore. The inaugural trips lasted some considerable time but all the boys displayed both confidence and aptitude.

Back at the campsite the Vesseys were leaving. They had enjoyed a wonderful week and were heading off next to the central highlands. They completed the visitor comments book with a lovely reference to the welcome they had received from both Phyllis and Reg and couldn't leave without an outstanding review of their trip to see the puffins. Yet more lovely people thought Phyllis as they made their way from the site. It was the visitors as well as the splendour of Camus that made her job so enjoyable indeed she hardly thought of it as a job at all.

Now that the Easter holidays had started, Phyllis couldn't wait to meet up again with the Coles. They had been some of their first visitors to Camus. Now it was their sixth season so Phyllis worked out that Max must by now be about nine. The daughters, probably about 19 and 21, were not coming this time. Phyllis expected that they were holidaying independently and probably in some sun-drenched destination.

They arrived with their large motor home followed, as expected; by Norman although Sue, being previously acquainted with Norman, paid heed to Reg's request to shut the gate. Phyllis went straight out to greet them even before they came into the reception.

"Well hello, it's so lovely to see you again" Phyllis said with real feeling "It's been a few years hasn't it? Come and say hello to Reg."

"Did you have a good drive?" Reg asked Graham.

"Yes not bad" came the reply "We stopped for a few days at Killin so we only had to do the last hop today. You must have been here for a few years now. When we came last it was your first season wasn't it?"

"Indeed it was" laughed Reg "This is now our sixth and we've been really busy. I'll have to show you the converted steading and the finished tractor when you've settled in."

Both Reg and Phyllis turned their attention to Max.

"My how you've grown" said Phyllis "Last time you were here you couldn't see over the counter."

Max was now a grown boy and seemed somewhat embarrassed by the attention which was now all directed at him.

"Do you remember being rescued by Angus?" asked Reg "It was certainly an eventful day and one I've never forgotten!"

Max smiled "Yes" he said "Dad hasn't brought the dinghy this time though."

They filled in the registration form and returned to their motor home to choose a pitch. There were plenty of pitches to choose from. Only the Willis's and the Mill's were on the caravan site. However this was the first weekend of the Easter school holidays and Phyllis was expecting more to arrive.

Having allowed the Coles to settle in, Reg was eager to show them the improvements that he had made over the past five seasons. The tour showed off the re-furbished toilet block, the steading, the new visitor information area, complete with the extended range of activities of both rough and clay pigeon shooting, ending the tour at the boathouse where there were just a few empty kayaks lying on the beach. Donnie was still out at sea with some of the students and the girls had wandered off for a while.

Max seemed really interested when he saw the kayaks. "Can I have a go?" he asked his dad.

"I'm not sure" replied Graham "Do you know the minimum age limit Reg?"

"I'm not sure but Donnie will know. I'll ask him when he gets back" replied Reg, feeling that he should have known that before he was asked.

Graham explained that they had chosen to come back at Easter rather than wait for the summer months because they were likely to avoid the dreaded midges. Reg agreed that as the midges normally start to arrive from May onwards, Easter was a good choice.

Donnie was pleased with the boys' trial trip across the bay. Tom was clearly competent but the others were also picking it up well. It was a lovely calm day and within the bay the water, like a sheet of glass, reflected the raised shoreline and the full colours of the rocky cliffs around. The grey jagged rocks, the dark peaty soil and the lichen-covered boulders all added to the tapestry on display. The kayaks gently broke the water's surface, leaving a trail, like an arrow, rippling gently and quietly into the distance. The boys had hoped to head across to the islands the following day but Donnie was not swayed. Not wishing to dampen their enthusiasm he went on to explain.

"Firstly, it is further than it looks" he said. "Then there's the effect of the current which you're not used to and, even if we get that far, the islands have huge, steep cliffs and there are only a few suitable beaches for the kayaks to get ashore."

The lads were disappointed but they accepted Donnie's suggestion that they took a day trip around the headland instead. To get the adrenaline pumping Donnie injected the idea that they could incorporate a few races, meeting with approval from them all.

Seeing Donnie back at the boathouse, Reg, Graham and Max had come down to meet him. Max remembered Donnie from all those years ago, especially the fishing trip they had all taken in Angus's boat.

"Well hello there" greeted Donnie "My you've grown up a lot Max."

"You too" responded Graham "We've been admiring your new venture and were wondering whether you could fit Max and myself in for a kayak lesson? I don't think I'll try a dinghy again after last time!"

"I'm taking the girls out this evening and then the boys again on a day trip tomorrow but I could take you on Monday, weather permitting. I need to give you both an induction before we go out. How old are you now Max?" asked Donnie.

"I'm nine, nearly ten." replied Max looking worried.

"The minimum age is eight so you'll be fine but we'll probably stay closer to the shore at first. I'm not sure that my dad would want to rescue you again from one of his buoys." Donnie's response was met with laughter from all.

During the afternoon a German couple were due to arrive with a pop-top Eriba, so Phyllis had stayed in the reception to wait for them. Fortunately they both spoke good English which always made Phyllis feel somewhat inadequate. She had considered taking up language lessons again. She was good at French in school but that was many years ago. During the previous seasons they had received visitors from Germany, Holland and France. Indeed it seemed a popular location especially with those from the Netherlands who loved the wild mountains, so different from the terrain back home. She encouraged the new arrivals to choose a pitch and promised to show them around once they were settled. Two families were also due in a few days so it was likely to be a busy period.

Phyllis was waiting for Reg to return when Drew, the postman called by.

"Hiya Drew" said Phyllis as he came into the reception "Yet more bills I expect."

"Mornin Phyllis" he replied. "No Reg today?"

"No he's just away round the site with the guests."

"It's beginning to look busy" Drew observed "Bookings good?"

"Yes, we've got 17 caravanners and more campers here by the end of the week so not too bad thanks" replied Phyllis.

One letter was from Annie, her daughter. Phyllis instantly recognised the handwriting. What could she be writing about? They spoke on the phone most weeks so it must be important. The letter started with the usual update about the grandchildren and what they were both up to. It then said that Annie's husband, Craig was applying for a job near Stirling. Just as she was beginning to immerse herself in her letter, Phyllis looked out, only to see that the German couple were now outside their van looking around. As a great host, she was torn between taking them on the promised tour, having a nose in their van or turning the page of her letter to read more.

Being the perfect hostess she quickly decided that the letter would just have to wait so she temporarily put it back in the reception drawer and went out to tend to her guests. The German's Eriba van was compact compared to the usual British van but inside showed a remarkable use of space.

There was a fixed bed to the rear, a washroom, a small kitchen and seating to the front. Everything you could need and an elevating roof giving more head room.

"I expect that it's easier to tow around these narrow lanes" remarked Phyllis.

"Yes and we can tow it with a smaller car because it's lighter" said Mr Amsel.

"Would you like me to show you around?" Phyllis asked.

"Yes please" replied Mrs Amsel "Could you also tell us about places to go and things to see?"

Phyllis's tour ended in the reception so that she could show them all the maps and leaflets about the area. She told them about the TV film due to be shown in a week's time. As they had booked for 10 days they would be able to watch it on the TV which Reg and Donnie were setting up in the steading. They took a number of leaflets from the reception back to their caravan to look through and seemed impressed with the variety of opportunities offered.

At last she was able to return to the drawer and immerse herself in Annie's letter. Craig had been working in mechanical engineering for some time but his job was at risk as a result of the recession. An opportunity had arisen for him to apply for a job in Stirling. Annie did not currently have a job as she had not returned to work since having William. Craig had sent off his application and was awaiting a reply. Stirling was quite a way from Camus but so much nearer than Worcester. They could make the journey easily in a day.

"I'm back" announced Reg as he reappeared in the reception.

"We've just got a letter from Annie and she might be moving to Scotland. I'm so excited Reg" blurted out Phyllis as she rushed over to give him a big hug.

She passed the letter to Reg whilst hovering excitedly to gauge his reaction.

"Well, they've only said that he's applied" said Reg with his calmer voice "It doesn't mean that he's got the job."

"Wouldn't it be great though to have them all nearer? I can't wait to tell Meg. The guests have all arrived now so can you hold the fort?" asked Phyllis.

"I can" replied Reg "but its early days yet. Don't get too excited."

Reg's advice fell on deaf ears. Phyllis was now on a mission and headed straight for Taigh Meg.

By the time Phyllis had pulled up on to the drive, Meg had spotted her and put the kettle on. Phyllis simply tapped on the door and pushed it open as she usually did. It was normal for folk to leave their doors and their cars unlocked, something unheard of back in Worcester. There was little or no crime here and open doors offered a welcome to guests so typical in these parts.

Meg had four B&B guests staying for a few days but as it was now late afternoon they were out and not expected back until tea time. As usual, Meg had baked a tempting home-made cake and the ladies were happy to partake, after all one simply couldn't refuse! Besides which, Meg's cakes always went down well with the endless conversation!

Phyllis couldn't hold back her exciting news.

"I've just received a letter from Annie. It looks like they could be moving to Stirling" she announced. "Craig's applied for a job. It will be great to have them all up here. I'll be able to see Ellie and William and you could tell them more stories about Norman."

Meg soon picked up on the excitement "When will they know for sure?" she asked.

"They didn't say" said Phyllis "But he's well qualified so he's sure to get it." Phyllis knew, deep down, that she was probably assuming too much but that did not dampen her mood.

The two ladies, fuelled by each other, talked about where the family might live and how lovely it would be for the children to grow up in Scotland. William would now be nearly nine months and Meg was starting to plan what she could bake for his first birthday party.

"Is Reg excited?" asked Meg.

"He's being a bit reserved, as usual. He thinks that Craig might not get the job but I've got this feeling. You know Meg. It's a mother's instinct" Phyllis replied, smiling at her friend's cheery face.

They seemed to talk for ages indulging in two cups of tea but when they checked the time it was nearly 5 o'clock. Annie would be back from school now and Phyllis was keen to ring her. Meg had promised her guests a chicken stew with dumplings so she also had good reason to bid her friend farewell.

As soon as Phyllis got back to Camus she rang Annie. The two loved to catch up with each other but as Annie was supervising the children's tea she wasn't able to say too much. Ellie was at the table and Annie was keen to keep everything low key so that Ellie wouldn't pick up on the fact that she would have to change schools, move house and everything that a young child might find daunting. Annie simply confirmed what was in her letter. The closing date for applications was at the end of the week so Annie promised to keep her updated.

It was a beautiful evening at Camus. Donnie had taken Megan and Carly along the coast in pursuit of otters. Max was skimming stones from the shore and his parents had settled down with a glass of wine or two. The students had organised a BBQ outside the steading, filling the site with the delightful aroma of sausages and venison burgers bought from the local butcher. As the two girls went off for the evening, the boys were left to fend for themselves.

Donnie's trip with the girls did not reveal any otters although there were clear signs of 'scat' or otter poo on some of the rocks. There were also half-eaten crab claws and empty mussel shells a little way from the campsite. Although the girls would have been delighted to see a wild otter, they really enjoyed their experience in the kayaks and promised to try again before the week was out. The sun was just beginning to lose its heat as it dropped lower to the west. The water was dead calm and reflected the early evening sky which seemed to increase in brightness and pick up the reflection of clouds passing overhead, like dabs of cotton wool.

Back at the caravan site, the mood was relaxed. Everyone was out enjoying the evening although, it being only April, some guests had elected to add an extra layer of clothing in order to stay out and watch the sunset.

Reg and Phyllis took the opportunity to take an evening stroll along the beach. This evening in particular, Phyllis looked forward to talking to Reg about Annie and Craig and how nice it would be if they were to move to Scotland. Reg tried again to temper her enthusiasm. He knew how disappointed she would be if Craig's application were unsuccessful. Secretly though Reg too was hopeful. He never let on but he did miss the children and grandchildren. He kept himself busy but in the quieter moments, in his shed, his thoughts would often go back to his family ties in Worcester. He never told Phyllis, of course. That would surely amount to a chink in his armour.

The boys' kayak trip on the Sunday was great fun. They set off, all five, in individual kayaks, making their way around the headland. Occasionally they stopped to set themselves up for a series of races. At first Donnie would win easily but Tom was always hot on his tail. Of course Donnie's boat was superior which, according to Tom, always accounted for his position. They were all intensely competitive probably coming from their rugby background. After three, testosterone-fuelled races the score was Donnie first in all three, Tom second in two of the races and Paul in the third, due apparently to Tom being deliberately held back by the Woozie Ozzie, who allegedly stole his line.

With the day's kayaking coming to an end, Donnie and the boys decided to paddle back to Camus. The mood was calm, boisterous energy now expelled. Donnie smiled to himself as he reflected upon the day's activities. Such incredible strength and endurance shown earlier was now replaced with contented expressions of awe as the boys paddled their boats through the water, heads turning from time to time, obviously admiring the immense beauty, nature at its best, as gentle waves rolled shore bound.

The moment of serenity was violently interrupted by a frenzy of sea birds, arriving without warning, having been attracted by a large pod of feeding dolphins. Although the action was a little way off, the boys could see the distinctive dorsal fins excitedly breaking the surface. They caught brief glimpses of the lighter belly emerging from the water and counted somewhere between 10 and 12 individuals. Donnie called to the boys that the dolphins were herding fish, his words rushed and slightly raised. It was not unusual for Donnie see these incredible mammals, but it was a rare moment when viewed from a kayak on a flat calm sea. The dolphins would disappear under the water, only to reappear with an awe-inspiring turn of speed and change of direction, each dolphin appearing to play its part in the co-ordinated effort. The screeching sound and diving from sea birds only served to intensify the mêlée. It was a fantastic, almost unbelievable treat for the boys. Paul had even been able to get a few pictures on his mobile. Donnie too could hardly believe his luck, what better advert for his growing enterprise!

Calm waters resumed and with long, gentle paddle strokes the boys skimmed back to shore. Until then the boys had thought that their kayak experience was one of the best experiences of their lives but now it was even more than that, truly exceptional. Returning to Camus their demeanour was both reflective and highly charged. They recounted their experience to Reg, Phyllis and any other passing guests. Tom made sure that he recorded every detail of the event on both Reg's wildlife board and in Phyllis's diary. Donnie was equally excited knowing that Paul's pictures would soon be posted on Facebook and studied by students not only in Loughborough but perhaps even on the other side of the world! Carly and Megan were green with envy when they saw Paul's pictures. Now they were even more determined to see an otter.

# THE ONLY WAY IS UP!

It was now Monday and the whole site was alive with talk of the dolphin sighting. Wildlife awareness was heightened just in time for the Coles to take to the water hoping that they too might be lucky. Sue had been understandably nervous about Graham and Max going kayaking. She still remembered how worried she was the last time they went out to sea. Graham's dinghy had only been allowed on lakes, near their home ever since. She insisted that, Graham was to take his mobile although he was again reluctant. She went down to the boathouse to see them off.

This time the trip went without a hitch. Donnie took them along the shore in one of the tandem kayaks thinking that Max would not have the stamina required for the trip on his own. Initially they kept to shallower water. Max absolutely loved it and seeing that he was a born natural, Donnie confidently took them further out. They were on the water for several hours looking for anything they could spot but sadly there were no dolphins to be seen.

Two more vans arrived in the afternoon, the pre-booked families, each with two children. They were friends and as the first caravan entered the site the gate was left open, allowing the other to follow on. However, whilst Phyllis was completing the check-in details with both families congregating in the reception, no-one noticed that Norman had seen his chance to sneak in through the fortuitously open gate. He made his way across to the steading wondering whether an odd pellet had been left lying around. The students were down by the boathouse watching Graham and Max taking their kayak lesson but the door of the steading had been closed. Norman just had to look through the new window but it appeared to be very different now. He couldn't resist extending his long tongue to the pane of glass leaving a smeary mess which would not please Reg. When both vans pulled forward to choose their spot, Phyllis could see Norman, now feasting on the grass across the site on the tent area. Knowing that she had to move him off the site before Reg came back, she filled her hand with pellets and marched off in pursuit. It was too late though - Norman had, once again, left his mark. A freshly deposited highland cow pat, all warm and steaming, had been left in a prime spot. Phyllis was initially reluctant to leave it for Donnie to remove but, after all, Norman was Angus's bull and she needed to get back to the reception to show the new guests around. She therefore decided to leave it and pretend that it hadn't happened on her watch!

Just as Phyllis was getting Annie's precious letter out for yet another read, the children came into the reception to choose a few sweets from the counter. Reluctantly Phyllis put the letter in the drawer and patiently waited for them to make their choices. The children were excited, eyes eagerly scanning the sweets display. Like most young children on their way to a holiday destination, they had probably spent far too long cooped up in the back of a car and now needed to release some of their energy. Phyllis guessed that the children were between six and nine, certainly all of primary school age. She asked their names. Martin, Larry, Robert and Wendy they blurted out although Phyllis knew that she would never remember.

"Can you show us around please?" politely asked the eldest.

"Of course young man" said Phyllis "Are your parents ready to be shown around the site?"

Phyllis went to the two neighbouring pitches where the caravans had parked up. They were the Davis family and the Chesunts both from the Wirral. Neither had been to Camus before so they needed to be shown all the facilities. Phyllis used the opportunity to find out more about them. The men were both builders and were work colleagues. Their names were Brett and Grant. Their wives, Debbie and Mandy, both worked part-time and the children went to the same school. They had been friends for years and regularly spent their holidays together. They had been attracted to Camus by the glorious pictures on the website and the opportunities to see the wildlife on Mull without the added cost of taking the caravans across on the ferry.

They loved the views, the boathouse and the kayaks, although most of the children, who were all desperate to have a go, were probably too young. Phyllis took them to the steading which, of course, was particularly a facility for the campers. She was however so proud of the finished building that she had to include it in every tour, even for caravanners.

As soon as Max had returned, he went down to the beach and the new children soon joined him. The lovely thing about caravan holidays is the freedom it offers to families. Max, in particular, welcomed the opportunity to mix with the others and they were soon heading off along the beach together looking for anything that they might see in the water. The adults enjoyed the quiet time on their own ensuring that the older children took care of the younger ones.

Next morning Phyllis awoke with her head full of thoughts of Annie's letter. Impatiently she wished it was the end of the week so that she would know for sure whether Craig's application had been successful. As usual she needed to open up the reception for 9 am and as she looked out from the window, briefly watching the birds visiting her feeders, she caught sight of the Mills' lovely caravan. "Oh my goodness, I forgot to ask Angus about Andy wanting to go fishing" she thought. With all the excitement of Annie's letter it had completely slipped her mind. Fortunately, it was just then that the sound of Angus's truck could be heard pulling on to the tarmac.

"Morning hen" came his usual greeting.

He had a big smile on his face but before Phyllis could reply with her latest news he simply had to spread the word.

"Norman's first calf of the year has just arrived and it's a boy!" he exclaimed coming round the counter to give her a big hug.

Angus's hugs were something else, like a big bear grasping you and squeezing the air out completely.

"Where's Reg? I need to tell him" he said, heading for the door.

"Before you go Angus I've got something to ask you." Phyllis said. "The young chap in the old caravan over there wants to know if you could take him fishing. I said that I'd ask what you thought."

Angus was still on his way out, keen to find Reg.

"I'll stop by and see him" said Angus who was obviously in a good obliging mood.

Reg was busy as usual, clearing out the old, dingy store attached to the toilet block, mindful to fit it out as a disabled wet-room hoping that this might meet with the approval from the tourist board and their impending visit. It would of course need a window to be installed and Reg had looked on the internet to see where he could source the required sanitary fittings.

"Hey Reg, what are you up to now?" called out Angus.

"Just planning the new disabled washroom" Reg replied from inside the store.

"Have you seen Norman lately?" Angus laughed. "He's become a dad again and it's a boy! We'll have to have a wee drammy later to celebrate."

"That's great news Angus. How many calves does that make it?" asked Reg as he emerged.

"Och, I'm not sure" the reply came "I'll have to look up the records. He's had loads born here but this one's a real beauty."

Angus had kept Tormad on the croft for nearly 15 years. He had serviced many cows which Angus bought at the Oban auctions. He had also earned his keep servicing the herds of many other breeders and those belonging to the neighbouring crofters. However Tormad was now getting older and it might well be time for a new bull, although Angus could never bear to sell him.

"I suppose that Phyllis told you our news" asked Reg assuming that Phyllis would have told him in the reception.

"Oh you mean your chap who wants to go fishing. I'll stop by his van in a while" said Angus leaving Reg somewhat puzzled.

"No, I mean the news about Annie. She and Craig might be moving to Scotland. Anyway, come in here and tell me what you think of this" he said, quickly changing the subject as he stepped back in to the dingy store. Reg was not inclined to say any more about Annie. He would wait until they had further news. At the moment seeing to the store was the focus of his attention and he was keen to seek Angus's, valued opinion.

On his way back, Angus stopped to talk to Andy. He had taken a couple of people fishing before but it was not something he did with any regularity. As he went out most days to check his creels it was no trouble to take another person on the boat. He told Andy that it was too early for the mackerel which were abundant off these shores from May onwards but that they may be lucky enough to catch a pollock or two. Andy confessed to being a newcomer to fishing but he'd love to give it a go. Just then, Angus spotted Graham and Max and couldn't resist saying hello.

"This man here knows all about fishing" Angus laughed as he shook Graham by the hand, literally!

"I say young man" he directed his words to Max "You're a bit bigger now. You must be eating too many tatties."

"Hello" replied Max quietly.

"What's that about fishing?" Graham asked.

"This man here, Andy isn't it?" continued Angus "He wants to go fishing on my boat. What do you think Max?"

"Do you think that we could come too?" asked Max, looking at his dad.

"Well if that would be ok Angus, we'd love to" replied Graham.

So Angus agreed that he would get back to them regarding which day and what time. He quite looked forward to it. The small contribution from the guests would certainly help to pay for the diesel.

Later that evening the children were all out and about and there was great interest in Max's kite which he took down to the beach. The wind had picked up a bit which meant that Max was able to keep the kite high in the air and also that the sound of the Willis's wind chimes was once again a regrettable feature of the site. It was lovely to see the children enjoying the outdoors and mixing so nicely. Max's kite was large, almost six feet across, with a curved wing shape and black, orange and yellow colours. It seemed that Max was quite good flying it or at least Phyllis assumed that it was Max as she watched from her window. Sue informed her that it was a Christmas present from his granddad and that he had been waiting to fly it on this holiday.

The Willis's and the Blunts appeared in the reception the very next morning to choose their activity for the day. The lighthouse was to be the destination for both families while Graham and Sue were planning to visit Fort William and check out Ben Nevis. Dependent upon the weather they might plan to climb it later in the week. It was now Tuesday and time for Donnie to take the boys out again with the Kayaks. Although the wind had picked up, he had seen their capabilities and thought it would be fine to take them out. The girls stayed behind, preferring to take a drive around the area and maybe check out Jimmy's ferry. The boys headed down to the boathouse not knowing how long they might be or how far Donnie would take them.

Andy and Sarah were preparing to go for a walk. They put on their walking boots and checked the Ordnance Survey map to plan a route around the coast. They came into the reception to buy some rolls so that they could take a picnic with them.

At 11am, Reg and Phyllis did their usual daily clean of the washrooms. It only took about half an hour after which Reg continued with his work in the store. Angus agreed on the size of the window which Reg had measured, although Angus knew that there would have to be good reason for him to disagree.

Reg asked Phyllis to order some supplies from Travis Perkins and she felt pleased that he asked her to spend some time choosing the colour schemes. The cost of any improvements was no longer met by Touring Haven Holidays. With this in mind Reg liked to make sure that he kept to a tight budget. He had, of course, spent a great deal of time on the internet. He had found Armitage Shanks very helpful and had received details from them of the requirements for disabled facilities along with suitable sanitary fittings, hand rails etc. They had not yet had any guests requiring wheelchair access but if they were to receive any enquiries it would be nice to offer appropriate facilities.

Sue, Graham and Max had left to head for Fort William, preparing for their ascent of Ben Nevis. It was a fair drive to Fort William and then a little further along Glen Nevis to the Ben Nevis Visitor Centre. Upon arrival they joined the long queue of tourists, all waiting to speak to a ranger.

Both Sue and Graham had done their fare share of peaks in the Lake District when they were a lot younger. Anticipating that the added years would make it harder this time, they were looking forward to the experience but not before seeking expert advice.

Just before them, in the queue, was a group of three young girls.

"Have any of you done much walking before?" asked the ranger.

"What do you mean?" they replied.

"Have you done Scafell or Snowdon for example?" he continued.

"No" came the reply followed by mutterings between them from which Sue could tell that they didn't have a clue what he was talking about.

The ranger concluded that Ben Nevis was not an undertaking to be taken lightly and Sue's thoughts naturally turned to her own girls, Charlotte and Natalie.

"I wanted to do this last time" Sue said to Graham "but there's no way the girls would have done it. I hope that they're having a good time in Lanzarote."

"I hope so too" said Graham "but I must say that I'm not missing them."

"Me neither" piped up Max "I can't wait to tell my friends that I've climbed the highest mountain in Britain."

Finally it was their turn. They asked the ranger how long it might take to reach the summit and what day was likely to be the best. The ranger advised that Thursday was likely to be good, offering clear views and only a slight threat of rain. The return trip following the 'Mountain Track' was likely to take about eight hours, excluding a rest at the summit. He asked if they had done much walking before, which indeed they had, and he told them that they should be fully prepared and bring different layers of clothing. At over 4000 feet it would be much colder at the top than it feels at the start. They were surprised at the suggestion that they should take two litres of water each to drink but accepted the advice and made sure that they popped into the supermarket on the way home to ensure that they were properly prepared.

Camus had more visitors arriving by the day. A few more campers came with tents and without exception they all seemed impressed with the steading. Some just pitched up overnight and others for a few days. They were mainly younger folk who spent the day walking but one plucky couple were well in their 60's. Phyllis booked them in whilst Donnie was out with the kayaks. They had been campers for the best part of 40 years and were well used to being cold and wet. They had been to most areas of Scotland and loved the Cairngorms but this year they had decided to head further west and explore. Ruth and Bernie were both retired now and although they used to have an old ridge tent they now enjoyed a modern Kyham tent with more headroom. Phyllis watched them from her window with admiration as they erected the tent, showing the experience they had clearly earned over many years.

The two families, the Davis's and the Chesunts, had been to the lighthouse as planned. The adults together with four, excited children climbed to the viewing point of the lighthouse in the hope of seeing some Minke whales or perhaps a basking shark. In truth it was almost certainly too early in the year; only from June onwards does the Gulf Stream bring vast quantities of plankton encouraging these ocean giants to feed off the West Coast.

The climb to the top of the tower involved 152 steps and was quite strenuous but the views at the top were amazing looking across to the Isle of Mull and, to the north, Skye, Muck, Eigg and Rhum. The lighthouse, built from granite from the Isle of Mull, had a pinkish hue. From the information centre they learned that it was no longer manned but was operated automatically, providing a vital navigational aid to ships around the West Coast. They made their way outside to the fog horn platform but, being April, here at the most westerly point of the mainland, it was too cold to scan the sea for long in the hope that they might spot something. Instead they made their way to the coffee shop and between them they enjoyed amazing carrot cake, several portions of coffee and walnut cake and huge chocolate brownies for the children. When they returned to Camus they gave good reviews of the cakes in the lighthouse café. The children were hoping to see Max again and fly his kite but he was not back yet.

When the Coles did pull onto the site the children resumed their games along the shore. Everyone seemed to be having a good time as the adults settled to a nice cup of tea. The older campers, Ruth and Bernie, took the opportunity to make full use of the washing and drying facilities offered in the steading as they had already been camping for a week and therefore had clothes to wash. They were quiet, unassuming guests who went out walking most days and Bernie put his name down for a spot of clay pigeon shooting with Reg.

Phyllis started to think ahead to the weekend and the screening of the TV film. It might be nice to organise a site BBQ outside the steading. The boys had brought a small BBQ which they had used the previous evening. Reg and Phyllis had one too. If Donnie could borrow one from Elaine and Angus then perhaps that would be enough. She had considered inquiring whether Reg could build one but he was busy with the new washroom and would almost certainly be irritated if she were to ask. Today was Tuesday and if she could get an idea of numbers she would be able to order meat from the butcher and more rolls from the baker.

She prepared a sign to put up in the reception asking guests to indicate their requirements by the end of Thursday.

Graham and Max enjoyed their Kayak trip on Monday and were looking forward to the planned fishing trip and then their ascent of Ben Nevis, which was scheduled for the Thursday. There was certainly so much to do here from the Camus base. Angus called by in the evening having checked the weather. He had found out that the forecast for Wednesday was light wind and low cloud, perfect for their plans. This fitted in nicely with Graham who now had plans for Thursday. Angus also checked with Andy and so it was agreed to meet at Angus's jetty at 4pm on the Wednesday. Angus would bring the bait and a few spare rods that they could use.

On the Wednesday afternoon Sarah sat outside her caravan, quietly enjoying her books and Sue took herself off to some visitor attractions including a wonderful craft shop selling yarns and buttons. It was one of her hobbies to make clothes for period dolls so she bought quite a variety of things which she knew she could use at some point. Mr and Mrs Willis only went out occasionally but usually returned with another decorative object to add to the awning. Reg simply couldn't believe it when he saw Mr Willis proudly erect a vibrant blue dolphin windsock high above his caravan. It must have been over 3ft from the top of the dolphin to the tip of its 'tail'. It adopted a pose as if it were splashing and jumping from the ocean. Presumably the long blue tails, designed to flutter in the breeze, were meant to depict the sea. The Willis's dog had been no problem. It too seemed an unnecessary object and was mainly seen sitting on Mrs Willis's lap on one of the sun loungers. He didn't go for many walks. He probably had everything he needed just where he was.

At 4pm on Wednesday the time came for Angus's fishing trip. As Donnie had no more people booked for kayak trips he decided to go too to help the guys with their tackle whilst his dad tended to the creels. Andy was a good laugh. He had read all the books on fishing before he came but obviously had no practical idea. He sat at the back of the boat waiting patiently but it was a long wait. Angus knew that the fish might be better round the headland but he had to collect the other creels first. He was clearly having more success than Andy as his first four creels contained two lobsters, each of a fair size.

"What do you do with the lobsters?" asked Graham.

"If I catch enough I take them across to the market in Tobermory but if it's only a few Jimmy buys them from me and Joyce prepares them for the restaurant" Angus replied.

"If you don't mind me asking Angus, how much do you get for each lobster?" enquired Graham

"Och recently it's been only about £7 per kilo at the market and I'll no get rich on that" he laughed.

Graham and Max were trying their luck with spinners but only managed to bring in a few small fish. After a while and with beginners' luck on his side Andy felt something on his line and shouted for Donnie's help.

"I think I've got something" he shouted "what do I do now?"

"You need to set your hook" was Donnie's reply.

"Do what?" Andy shouted in excitement.

Donnie made his way to the side of the boat where Andy was fishing and told him to give his line a quick jerk backwards and upwards explaining that this would ensure that hook takes hold. Andy, somewhat panic stricken, did as he was told and immediately the line started to move erratically through the water.

"Keep the line tight. Lift up the rod and slowly reel it in, keeping it tight. You don't want to lose this one" Donnie was giving advice all the time.

The fish put up quite a struggle. It seemed like it would be a good size. Donnie quickly got his landing net and after a short while the slippery, silver fish emerged from the water and plopped in to the net. Donnie identified it as a pollock, a member of the cod family. Andy was surprised to see that in spite of the apparent struggle it was less than a foot in length but that didn't matter. It was his first catch and he was proud and excited. He raised his hand to all on board to exchange high fives and hurriedly searched for his camera.

"Not a lot of eating there" said Donnie. "Do you want to throw it back?"

"Wait a minute" replied Andy "must get a picture first".

Donnie helped him to extract the hook and he proudly held his catch aloft for the expected photo with the others all gathered round. As it was not big enough to take back to Camus, Angus kept it to use as bait for his creels.

After Angus had collected his creels he had managed to keep a total of six lobsters. The creels had trapped several more but, after measuring them, most had to be thrown back in as they were below the minimum size. He would take his catch to Joyce the next morning, for serving up in the boathouse. All the boys had thoroughly enjoyed their fishing trip and returned with big smiles on their faces.

Andy rushed back to his caravan like an excited boy. He couldn't wait to show Sarah the pictures on his camera.

"It was this big" he blurted out making the gesture of size with a spread of his hands as was normally expected from a fisherman.

Sarah laughed hysterically. "Well where is it then?" she asked.

"We gave it to Angus" Andy answered.

"Thank god you didn't bring it back here" she said "I wouldn't have known what to do with it."

"Well you'll have to find out" Andy laughed "I've got a feeling that I'm going to be good at this."

As a novice fisherman, Andy was obviously delighted with his result. He hadn't yet spent many cold, wet, fruitless hours on a boat or on the shore to dampen his enthusiasm.

Thursday came and it was time for the Coles to head towards Ben Nevis. They made an early start, planning to get there for 8.30am and hopefully back down by 4.30pm. It was a lovely day, the sun was out and it was warm once they got going. The ascent started well, relatively smooth. The ranger had told them that 'The Mountain Track' was renamed in 2004. Prior to this it was known as 'The Tourist Route' but the change of name was a deliberate attempt to deter the unwary visitor and make them aware that this was indeed a serious walk, hardly a walk in the park.

A bridge took them across from the visitor centre to the west side of Glen Nevis. At first the track meandered through the lush green valley, becoming steeper quite rapidly. They were able to look around, taking in the beauty and appreciating the views in all directions. Quite frequently there were large steps made from huge boulders buried deep in to the ground. These were known as 'Granny blockers' presumably intended to encourage any who might already be struggling to turn back. Sue and Graham were determined to continue although they were stopping periodically for some of the water that they were reluctantly carrying; the warmth from the sun made them appreciate the refreshment. Max was steaming on ahead with youth on his side. The route was surprisingly busy with walkers, mainly younger but some older, many going at a faster pace than Sue but then she was enjoying the vistas. For her it was not so much a matter of time but more the whole experience that she enjoyed. She couldn't help but notice that many of the youngsters were dressed in shorts and a t-shirt with no sign of a back pack containing fleeces or jackets. Several only carried a small bottle of pop or water and not the two litres they had been advised to carry. Her own girls were of a similar age and her motherly instincts wanted to stop them and check that they were suitably prepared but she knew that young people always thought they knew best. They were unlikely to react favourably to her intervention. It was nice, however, to see so many young people enjoying the outdoors, something she had never managed to do with her daughters.

At the half way point the land had thankfully flattened out, giving already tired legs a chance to recover. It was still well before midday but nevertheless they agreed that it was time to break out the sandwiches which Sue had prepared the previous evening. Judging by the spent banana skins and the odd empty drinks bottle, it was obviously a favourite spot for others to stop. Sue was hoping that there might be somewhere suitable to go for a wee but there was little opportunity. There were no trees or bushes and only a few indiscreet rocks; she therefore pushed the thoughts to the back of her mind. The views were already amazing but they knew that there was much further to go so after only a 20 minute rest they were soon on their way again.

The terrain was changing; the green glen was now replaced by a more barren, stony path continuing to ascend in a series of large zigzags. They were still on the west flank of The Ben as the locals had fondly named it. The ascent was gradual but arduous, reflecting the fact that it was originally followed by ponies taking supplies to the now abandoned observatory at the top. Neither Sue nor Graham had yet seen the summit but they frequently asked each other whose crazy idea this had been.

As they approached the summit they spotted areas of snow which often persisted right through the year. It had been quite warm at the start of their walk but they were now grateful to stop and get out the fleeces they had been carrying in their back packs. At one point on the route there was a sheltered hollow, completely covered by hard packed snow, never being given the opportunity to thaw. Max and Graham had to help Sue across the ice which was slippery from the tramping of hundreds of feet.

As they reached the summit they could not believe the numbers who were already there, many taking photos of their friends waving at the large cairn marking the trig point. Sue wanted a photo of Max and Graham but another climber intervened to ask whether they would like a photo of them all together. Sue, of course, agreed. It turned out that he was a student from Edinburgh University climbing The Ben to raise money for cancer care. Sue congratulated him and got Graham to get £5 from his wallet to add to the charity funds.

Having reached the summit, Sue was keen to check out the observatory. Only a few ruined walls remained but the ground was difficult, covered in loose rocks and it was obvious, judging by the discarded scraps of tissue, that many climbers had used the shelter provided for a much welcome relief! All in all it was not the most pleasant place to stop and reflect on their achievement.

They returned to the edge of the plateau, looking across to admire the views. Briefly they could see the infamous North Face, the ascent preferred by serious climbers. The North Face was soon obscured however by a snow storm moving swiftly across. Once again the Coles dug down in to their back packs, bringing out the all-weather jackets they had brought. Others tried to seek shelter behind the rocks or scurry back down the mountain like a hoard of scared lemmings. Graham could clearly see how the mountain rescue volunteers frequently had their work cut out, envisaging ill-prepared visitors twisting ankles in their haste to descend.

Being at the summit, Sue decided to send a text to Charlotte and Natalie sending her love from the highest mountain in Britain but the text did not send. How was that possible? They started to head back, taking great care to cross the already snow-covered gullies, now made even more treacherous by the fresh flakes. It was 3pm and their thoughts of making it back down by 4.30 looked rather optimistic. Once they were off the plateau, the snow stopped and the temperature was noticeably getting better. Still near to the top they looked down through the wispy clouds only to see a military aircraft passing below them. It was not quick like a fighter jet but slower, possibly a troop carrier. It made its way down the glen between the mountains and was in view for quite a while.

"What an experience!" exclaimed Graham." I've never looked down upon an aircraft before. Just look at it Max."

Max was already rooted to the spot preparing to take yet another amazing picture to add to his holiday album.

Sadly the only route down was the same as the way up and Sue was soon realising that going downhill seemed just as much hard work as it was going up, if not harder. Their progress was slow, probably due to tiredness, but as they made their way back Sue heard the recognisable sound from her mobile indicating that, at last, her message, sent at the summit, had finally got a signal. Until then they had obviously been too high for the nearest transmitter to pick it up. Sue clearly still had a lot to learn about text messaging.

After what seemed like a long descent, they once again saw the welcome sight of the green glen below. Their thoughts turned to Camus and what they might eat that evening. It was 6.30pm when they got back to their car, a full 10 hours since they left. The warden's estimate of eight hours must have been based on the younger, fitter ramblers. They therefore decided to stop at the Ben Nevis Inn for dinner as they still had an hour's journey to get back to

Camus. The Inn was not just a welcome relief from the exertion expelled throughout their memorable day but the simple haggis, neeps and tatties was a hearty, fitting end. Sue took the trouble to ring Phyllis to let her know that they would be back later. She really didn't want to trouble Phyllis and Reg again and encourage yet another search party. They finally returned to Camus at 9.30pm. All three slept well with no sign of life from their caravan until well in to the following morning.

The week was disappearing fast and the good weather was also changing. There were more clouds and the wind was once again increasing. The Willis's dolphin was doing its best to hang on and, according to Reg, the wind chimes were fast becoming wind irritations. Phyllis immersed herself with the forthcoming BBQ. There were 30 guests from the site intending to come. She hoped that the evening would stay dry and needed to arrange the orders with the butcher and baker.

Sarah and Andy meanwhile had been to Jimmy's ferry. Whilst they were there they arranged a trip to Mull and met up with Ruth and Bernie, who were also booking the same trip. Phyllis had phoned Joyce to ask her to the BBQ on Saturday. She was delighted to accept and said that they would be over as soon as the ferry was back. Meg was coming too, as were Angus, Elaine, Paige, Camran and Donnie.

The eagerly awaited evening arrived. Angus agreed to stay outside and help Reg with the BBQ as it would be a push to get everyone in the steading. The caravanners helped by bringing extra chairs from their vans or awnings which they squeezed around the table whilst Phyllis's long benches were moved to the front for the children to share. The atmosphere was like a party, with everyone exchanging stories of where they'd been, what they'd seen and other sites they had also visited. Guests brought bottles of wine and pop ready to share a good evening.

The TV programme lasted for 40 minutes and, from outside, Phyllis could hear the excitement as they saw familiar landmarks around the site and the activity around her bird tables. The opening scenes panned around the tranquil site with the views to die for. Of course, Norman was at last on film, captured typically on the bridge, a real superstar!

The BBQ was timed to be ready before the film but those who had seen it before would be served later. After the show, Donnie continued the evening with some lively music and everyone spilled outside to enjoy the beautiful sunset which was sure to be the icing on the cake! In April the sun would set between 8pm and 9pm and as the film had started at 7.00pm they all made their way out by 7.45pm allowing plenty of time to see the sky turning a bright golden colour across the bay. The children continued to run around playing, whilst many of the adults returned to their vans or tents in search of cameras to capture the spectacle.

As evening advanced couples were holding hands, sharing discreet embraces as the natural world played out its final act of the day, charged with immense pride, even Reg pecked a quick kiss on Phyllis's lips. As if scripted, the sun lit up the clouds, giving them a distinct golden back drop, gradually piercing through, shedding vivid yellow streaks of colour across the water. As the sun sank lower on the horizon, the golden glow changed to deep orange, gradually becoming a burning crimson as it was finally swallowed from view.

# WHO'S A PRETTY BOY THEN?

Phyllis was on the phone to Annie on a daily basis checking whether Craig had heard anything but there was nothing to report yet. As the following week started, several of their guests were due to leave. The Coles and the students moved on and by the end of the week it was time for the Willis's to pack up their considerable belongings. Phyllis watched the well-rehearsed routine. Throughout their stay at Camus, the Willis's had acquired even more 'essential' items - two storm straps and a dolphin wind sock. Her observations were however interrupted when, on the Friday, Annie rang excitedly to tell them that Craig had indeed been shortlisted and had been invited to an interview. Ellie would have gone back to school by then so Craig would have to go on his own to Stirling, by train. He wasn't planning to come to Camus this time but they had booked a room at Meg's for two weeks in the summer.

Phyllis's excitement would therefore have to be contained a little longer but the Tourist Board were expected on 27th so there was much to do to make sure that the site was all ship-shape.

Camus was getting busier with new guests, new faces and different characters. Phyllis took on more of the regular tasks, leaving Reg to finish off the disabled washroom. As usual he paid a great deal of attention to detail. He had not allowed Phyllis to see it until it was completely finished but when she was finally invited in, she had to admit that, even for Reg, the overall impression was amazing. The floor was a contemporary grey and the wall tiles white with a grey border. The sink and mirrors were set at the correct height for a wheelchair user. She was so very proud of her husband's efforts and hoped that it would suitably impress the Tourist Board officials. Having completed the new washroom, Reg was straight on to the hard-standings and hook-ups. He cleared away any large stones and used his roller to level out the land, ordering the requisite amount of 20ml gravel, enough to spruce up a dozen pitches.

Phyllis attended to her floral displays. Many of the spring bulbs were now spent but the tulips and daffodils were hanging on. The summer bedding plants were not yet ready to be put outside but she had bought a few cloches and was protecting her overwintered begonia tubers, ready to start the main display.

Entries had been made in the wildlife diary by many visitors over the Easter holidays. It was important to have it prominently on display in the information area alongside the posters prepared by the Tourist Board. The comments written in the visitor book were very complimentary so Phyllis ensured that it was in a prime position on the front desk. The items available from the site shop were neatly stacked on one side of the reception; not only the essential food and toiletry items but also advice as to where, in the local village, more items could be sourced. There was also a clear sign of the stock held in Reg's store, for example gas bottles, chemicals for caravan toilets, awning and tent pegs.

Each time that the phone rang Phyllis was hopeful that it would be Annie but although she was happy to receive further enquiries and bookings, most calls were from visitors making reservations. It was at the end of the day, just as Phyllis was leaving the reception, that phone rang and a familiar little voice was on the end of the line.

"Hello nanny, guess what? We're coming to live near you soon," Ellie announced very excited and giggly.

"Oh won't that be just wonderful. I'm all excited too" replied Phyllis "I can't wait to tell Granddad and Meg."

"I'm going to go to school in Scotland" Ellie continued with no hint of sadness. "We'll be able to do lots and lots and I'm going to be able to see Norman whenever I want."

"Has mummy told you that Norman has a baby? He's all fluffy at the moment and he's very cute" Phyllis told her.

"What's he called?" asked Ellie.

"I don't think he's got a name yet. Angus has said that I can choose one, perhaps you could help me. Is Mummy there? I expect that Mummy and Daddy are all excited too!"

Ellie passed the phone to Annie. Phyllis could hear her granddaughter running away and laughing. Annie confirmed that Craig had been offered the job, subject to references etc. The company would be looking for him to start in June. She and Craig needed to put their house up for sale and start looking for a place near Stirling. The new company would pay for rented accommodation for up to four months which would be really handy. Annie also needed to find a school for Ellie but thought that it might be better to start her after the summer holidays. Phyllis had so many questions to ask. She was keen to help. Did Annie want her to look at schools, houses etc? These days, with the internet, Annie would do her own research but they would almost certainly come up for the Whitsun half term to look around.

Annie needed to get the children in the bath and suspected that it might take some time to calm them down so she ended the call, promising that she would ring back later. Phyllis hurriedly locked the reception and sped off to find Reg. She told him that Ellie had just been on the phone and that Craig had got the job. She intended to phone Meg but for now she would go and get their dinner started; tonight they would celebrate with a bottle of wine.

Over dinner Reg and Phyllis discussed Annie's move. Naturally this prompted them to consider selling their Worcester bungalow, conscious that it was now looking sad and tired and the windows, previously repainted every two years, were beginning to show the first tiny cracks in the paint, a sign that the frames would soon be weathered. Reg was only at the bungalow between November and February which was not suitable for external work. The garden also revealed the tell-tale signs of neglect. The bushes had been pruned to a fashion by a local gardener and the grass mowed at varying intervals but the manicured lawn which was Reg's pride and joy was now full of moss. The regular hedgehog inhabitants, who Phyllis used to feed each evening, had sadly now moved on. She loved to watch them sneaking out from the bushes onto the patio in search of food. She became quite fond of them and had even named them 'Pin' and 'Cushion'. The décor inside the bungalow was a little dated and they both felt that their hearts were now settled at Camus and they no longer missed the familiar streets and faces of Worcester. They had become accustomed to a very different life away from the weekly supermarket trip and the regular visits to the library. The locals around Camus had well and truly welcomed them into the community and their new friendships were deep. Now that Annie, Craig and the grandchildren were heading to Scotland there was very little reason to keep their home in Worcester. Somehow it all seemed like a distant memory.

They still loved their eight months of the year in their caravan but the winter months would surely demand something more substantial. They were fortunately both still in good health but the next big birthdays would see them turning seventy and they therefore needed to consider their future and a life of proper retirement, albeit still a few years off.          Reg had extended the lease of the land with Hamish for three years but perhaps it was worth considering something more permanent.

It was now getting late and they needed to be up early as they were expecting more guests. Phyllis hoped that the guests would all be really pleasant, helping to add to the overall impression for the Tourist Board during the following week.

The first to arrive was a party of campers from a church group in the Midlands. They arrived in two minibuses and a number of separate cars. They asked if they would be able to set up some larger marquees for prayer meetings and group activities to which Reg and Donnie agreed. In total there were 20 campers of mixed ages in the party, including one young man in a wheelchair. How timely it was, thought Reg, who was looking forward to having a real use for his new disabled wet room.

A few other guests arrived, including a middle-aged couple from Norfolk with their caravan and a husband and wife from Aberdeen in a motor home. Phyllis welcomed them all as usual and waited to give them a tour of the site. Reg had gone with Donnie to help the church party to set up their marquees. Finding the best, flat spot for the large tents took some time but Reg, armed with his cordless Dewalt, was able to take part and easily secure the pegs in to the ground. The party all pulled together like a well-oiled machine. Chris, the young man in the wheelchair, directed the team, including Reg, and acknowledging the vital role that Chris had been given, Reg adhered to his polite instructions and, for once, assumed a subservient role. The structure was secured and the large tarpaulin was tied in place. The whole process took quite a while but the mood of the party was great, kind and co-operative in contrast to the arguments often occurring between couples erecting their awnings.

Phyllis meanwhile, had been watching from her window for her opportunity to show the new caravanners round. The first couple to get settled were Bill and Brenda from Aberdeen. As Phyllis wandered across the site, she could hear a very unusual bird sound, a loud squawking, which she could not attribute to any of the local birds. She looked around, puzzled, but continued towards their van. As she came closer to their awning the sound became louder. Seeing the look on her face, Bill stepped out of his van smiling.

"You'll have to forgive Nigel" he said "He gets excited when we set up somewhere new but he'll quieten down in a while."

"Who's Nigel?" asked Phyllis.

Bill closed the caravan door behind him and immediately tapped as if he were seeking entry.

"Come in" squawked Nigel.

Phyllis's attention was directed at the window, through which she could see a beautiful grey parrot in its cage.

"That's Nigel" he said quite proudly "We take him everywhere with us. He's got to be the most travelled parrot I know."

"He's our baby" added Brenda "But he only likes men or me when I feed him, otherwise he bites! He loves the caravan - and the awning if it's not too breezy."

"So he talks" remarked Phyllis "How funny is that!"

"The trouble is people believe him. Try knocking on the door again" suggested Brenda.

Phyllis rapped her knuckles gently on the door.

"Come in" came the clear reply making Phyllis laugh again.

"Back home he told the gas man to come in to our house when I was still in the shower!" continued Brenda. "The gas man seemed a bit surprised when he came in only to find the rooms empty."

"What else does he say?" asked Phyllis now rooted with interest.

"He asks visitors if they want a cup of coffee, he calls Bill when its time for dinner, he asks me what I'm doing and also, when it's evening, he tells us that its time for 'drinkies'.

"He even mimics the reversing bleeps of the motor home" continued Bill "and I'm embarrassed to say that he is prone to road rage."

"That's because he copies you cursing the other drivers" sniggered Brenda.

They seemed to be there for ages recounting the stories of Nigel. Phyllis had almost forgotten that she had other guests to see but eventually she offered to show them round, asking whether Nigel would like to join them. Bill declined. Nigel's wings were clipped so there was no risk of him flying off but he was likely to add a few words of his own to Phyllis's repertoire and Bill didn't want him to offend.

Bill, Brenda and Nigel settled in quickly. Nigel was a star throughout the following week and a real attraction for all the other visitors. The couple, together with the parrot, ventured out in their motor home most days but not for any great distance. Prompted by Phyllis, Reg had also paid them a visit to meet Nigel and hear his rendition of the motor home reversing. They had been introduced to many dogs through the various seasons but never before had they had a visiting parrot. Angus was amused too.

"I expect that's a visit you won't want to be repeated!" he joked with Phyllis in reception, laughing his head off as he went out. Phyllis wasn't always quick at getting Angus's jokes but this time she could see the funny side.

Then there was the couple from Norfolk. Soon after their arrival Phyllis went to conduct her usual tour but as she approached their awning, she could hear them arguing and wondered whether she should politely walk away but just as she was hesitating Mrs Chisholm poked her head out. She had a beaming smile and a very posh voice.

"Hello there" she called to Phyllis. "Have you come to show us round?"

"Yes" replied Phyllis "if it's convenient. I could always come back later if you wish."

"No, right now would be just fine" Mrs Chisholm turned her head towards their van and snapped at her husband "Do hurry up dear, the lady is ready to show us round."

"He always does this" she continued stepping out of the awning "he has to check that everything is still secure in the cupboards after the journey. He's a real creature of habit."

Mr Chisholm emerged, not the down-trodden image that Phyllis had envisaged but diminutive in size just the same. They all walked around the site together, visiting the toilet block, the steading and the boathouse. Mrs Chisholm commented that she might enjoy 'a spot of canoeing' but her husband was not so sure.

"You know how you hate to get your clothes wet" he sighed.

"Yes but there is a washing machine in the hut" she replied. "Why are you always so negative? I just want to try out everything while we are here."

This was the first time that Phyllis had heard anyone refer to the steading as 'a hut'. She felt instantly offended and compelled to tell them about its history and how they had converted it with the help of her son.

As they returned to their caravan, Phyllis noted that they had foldable bicycles.

"Oh you plan to go cycling?" Phyllis remarked.

"We love to explore" replied Mr Chisholm. "Do you have any local maps only my wife so often gets us lost!"

"Oh you do exaggerate Rory". Mrs Chisholm was quick to correct him "You always refer to that one time in the Peak District which was not entirely my fault."

Phyllis suggested that they come to the reception where she had maps of the local area, assuring them that there were only a few roads around Camus therefore it was difficult to get lost, unless they intended to cycle for miles. She made her excuse to allow them to settle in. Normally she would have been reluctant to leave but, on this occasion, she was quite glad to get away from their niggles.

On the dry days, the Chisholms headed off on their cycles, having argued each time about the route they planned to take. It hardly seemed that there was much to argue about but they always seemed to manage it. They also booked a kayak trip, drawing Donnie in to the inevitable row.

"I think that it would be better to take the two person boat" said Mrs Chisholm introducing herself as 'Sue'.

"Well I'd prefer to row on my own" replied her husband Rory.

"If there are two of us rowing it might be easier" suggested Sue.

Donnie diplomatically said that it was entirely their decision. They only wanted to stay close to the shore so it really didn't matter. Mr Chisholm was insistent however on separate craft and Sue reluctantly agreed. Donnie thought that Mr Chisholm probably wanted to ensure that there was a reasonable distance between himself and his nagging wife and looked forward to an opportunity for peace and quiet. The couple were at the boathouse for half an hour before they finally selected a small kayak each before going out for the usual induction, followed by a good two hour trip, always hugging the shore line. They thoroughly enjoyed it although Rory was repeatedly shouting out instructions to Sue in an attempt to keep her on a straight course.

"Keep to the right" he shouted "You're cutting across my line."

"I most certainly am not!" replied Sue quite indignantly "It's you who's not keeping straight."

By the time they returned to the boathouse, Donnie looked completely drained.

The week was passing quickly. It was now Wednesday and the Tourist Board were due to arrive. Reg and Phyllis were up early making sure that the site was clean and tidy and that their guests were well catered for. It was a lovely bright day and several members of the church party were down at the boathouse embarking upon a kayak trip. There were 10 caravans and two motor homes on site, with the church party and three other tents pitched up. It therefore looked quite busy considering that it was still the 'low' season. Phyllis had planned for themselves and the Tourist Board officials to have lunch in the steading, having checked beforehand that no campers intended to use it. She had made a selection of rolls and Meg had baked some scrumptious scones the previous day which Phyllis had also laid out. She felt strangely nervous although, on the phone, the lady had told them to just be themselves. Reg, although always smart, made sure that he was particularly well turned out, polishing his boots the previous evening. Phyllis did her daily dead-heading of each of the troughs and filled the bird feeders to the brim.

It was almost midday when a Land Rover pulled onto the site with three people inside. Reg and Phyllis came out from the reception to greet them. As Reg shook hands and introduced both himself and Phyllis, they in turn responded with their names.

"I'm Rab" said the older man, "this is Laura and we've bought young Willie with us. I hope you don't mind but he's training to be an inspector so he's going to see what we do."

"Well it's lovely for you all to be here. We hope that we're not going to disappoint you Willie" said Reg with his usual confidence.

"Would you like a cup of tea?" asked Phyllis taking the orders and returning to the reception to put the kettle on.

"Come inside" gestured Reg stepping aside and pointing his arm towards the office.

"I must say that the drive here was wonderful, mind you it's a nice day. I don't suppose it's always like this" Rab laughed.

"I've been looking out for suitable places for the brown signs" interrupted Willie.

"We can't make the decision regarding the signs, Highways have to do that" advised Laura "but we can suggest suitable locations."

"Yes, I know" replied Reg who had thoroughly researched this on the internet. "Where do you think would be best Willie?"

"I think that there should be a sign just as you go through the main town and another before the village, oh and a further sign where you reach that fork in the road. I was trying to imagine where the signs would be most helpful" Willie replied with much enthusiasm.

After their tea, Rab told Reg and Phyllis that the inspection would last a couple of hours. They would start with a tour of the site then follow up with a more detailed inspection of the facilities and they would like Phyllis to show them some of the books from the reception. Of course Reg and Phyllis were welcome to ask any questions which they had. Phyllis immediately asked at what time they would like to share the lunch that she had prepared. Everyone agreed that they would conduct their tour first and have lunch later, after which they could all sit down together to complete the questionnaire.

Phyllis remained in the reception leaving Reg to take them back outside to start the escorted tour. Phyllis was pleased to see Laura pointing towards the coloured troughs with a smile on her face. Hopefully the smiles would continue throughout the day.

Reg made his way around the site starting with the caravan pitches. The guests who were still on site greeted him with "good afternoon Reg". When he reached the awning belonging to Bill and Brenda the group stopped, amused by Nigel's question of "what are you doing?" They admitted that this was the first time that they had met a parrot during one of their inspections. The tour continued with Reg taking them next to the boathouse where Donnie was busy with the campers. They seemed to stay there for ages, asking some of the visitors how the experience was going. After being shown the toilet block, they made their way to Reg's store where he took great pride in revealing his immaculate collection of tools and neatly stored supplies. Then it was on to the camping field and the converted steading, which was clearly the 'piece de resistance'. At this point they were not taking notes but Laura told Reg that, after their tour, they would like to go round again, on their own, and complete the necessary paperwork. In all they were gone for almost an hour when Reg returned, on his own, leaving the inspectors to their business.

"How do you think its going?" asked Phyllis nervously.

"Not bad" replied Reg "They were quite taken by Nigel and seemed to love the steading. I've left them on their own now.

"Will they give us a decision today?"

"I'm not sure" said Reg "I didn't want to pressure them."

Just then the bleep from the disabled toilet sounded and as Reg was hastily making his way outside, Willie came towards him to advise him that they were testing the pull cord. The assistance cord set off a flashing red light outside the washroom. Reg's speedy reaction was a good sign.

During lunch the discussion involved their history since taking on the site, their bungalow at Worcester and their plans for the future. Phyllis told them how excited she was that their daughter and grandchildren would be coming to Scotland soon and how much Ellie loved the wildlife. This brought them to the subject of the recent wildlife film and the encouraging responses received at the Tourist Information offices. The inspectors were looking forward to seeing the wildlife diary entries which had been made by the Camus guests. After lunch they returned to the reception to look at the history of bookings and the well-stocked display of leaflets and information. The inspectors had brought with them some details of attractions further afield, reminding Reg and Phyllis that a stay at Camus may well be only part of their guests' touring holiday and told them that details of

Camus had, similarly, been made available to other offices throughout Scotland.

They were clearly most impressed by the steading and the way it had been converted. Reg told them about how he had cleared it out and the objects that he had found, the most intriguing of which were the limpet shells. He went on to explain how he had found hundreds, many of which had been placed one inside another and he took the opportunity to ask them whether they knew any more about limpet shells from their visits to other former crofts. Neither Rab nor Laura knew much although they had heard that people in the highlands had eaten limpets when times were hard and that some very old sites in Scotland had also revealed limpet shells during archaeological digs. They suggested that Reg might find out more from the internet.

The inspectors now turned their attention to Donnie, asking if it would be possible for them to have a few minutes with him. Reg could see that the church party had returned from their kayak lesson and Donnie was putting away all the equipment.

"I'll go and ask" promised Reg, eager to oblige.

The Tourist Board had been very supportive of Donnie's business and had been a very useful source of advice and also finance. Rab was keen to find out how Donnie had spent the money received from the 'Growth Fund'. He had used it partly to improve the website and partly to cover the costs of training courses he had undertaken before the start of the season. He had brought along copies of the various certificates awarded. He had also spent some of the money buying further kayaks suited to the more experienced customers.

Reg and Phyllis were hoping that either Rab or Laura would give them some feedback before they left. They were not disappointed. While Rab spent time with Donnie, Laura returned to tell them that whilst officially they would have to await the formal confirmation in writing, they were going to award them three stars.

She handed them details of the Tourist Board gradings i.e.

1 star: clean and tidy, a fair and acceptable, if basic, standard
2 stars: a good overall standard
3 stars: a very good standard
4 stars: an excellent standard
5 stars: an exceptional standard

It was agreed that the facilities were of a very good standard and the things preventing them from achieving 4 stars were the insufficient number of hard-standings, the fact that there was no children's play area and the absence of a dedicated washing-up station. They also needed to accept payment by card for both the use of the site and also the kayaks. Laura assured them that the Tourist Board would assist them with the introduction of chip and pin technology.

Reg and Phyllis were really pleased with the award of three stars and even more spurred on by the seemingly minor requirements to reach four. The inspectors finally left just before five o'clock, leaving everyone relaxed and on a high. Phyllis couldn't wait to tell Elaine who would no doubt hear the news from Donnie when he went home. Elaine suggested that perhaps on Saturday, if the weather was fine, herself, Angus and the children would come along for a BBQ to celebrate. Donnie would invite a few of his friends and of course Meg was to be included as always. The news of the improved Tourist Board grading spread through the village like wild fire. It was the hot topic of conversation. All Reg and Phyllis now had to do was await the official confirmation.

# WHERE THERE'S A WILL!

It was now the last weekend in April. Reg and Phyllis were looking forward to meeting some new visitors and, in particular, to see the return of their good friends, Mick and Maureen. Phyllis was eager to catch up with Maureen and find out what she was planning to paint this time. It would be lovely if she could do a picture of the steading. On their last visit Maureen had asked Reg whether she could sketch Fergal, the now lovingly restored tractor. Phyllis had an idea that she could commission a painting of Fergal with the wonderful backdrop of the sea and distant islands beyond. If she were able to keep it a secret she could keep it as a present for Reg for their Ruby wedding anniversary on 2nd June.

A new couple pulled onto the site with a quite unusual outfit. They had a fairly large caravan, towed by a brand new VW Campervan. During the previous seasons, Reg had witnessed many a strange outfit including works transit vans towing caravans, ambulances converted to motor homes and some cars surely underpowered for the size of caravan. The sight of this smart outfit however was worthy of further investigation. Phyllis welcomed the couple as they completed their registration. They were Mr and Mrs Grant from London. Phyllis quickly noticed that Mrs Grant had difficulty with walking but as the couple said nothing she felt that she should not mention it. They left the reception and drove off to choose a pitch. Mrs Grant was slight but her husband was strong and well-built, over six feet Phyllis guessed. As Phyllis watched from her window, she noticed that Mr Grant was busying himself setting up the caravan whilst Mrs Grant was organising everything inside. After a while her husband offered his support as she made her way gingerly outside. Phyllis thought that she should go and see if they needed any help. As she approached their pitch Mrs Grant came over to see her.

"Hello again" said Phyllis "I thought that I'd pop over to check that everything is ok."

"Yes fine thank you" replied a cheerful Mrs Grant "What beautiful views you have here".

The tailgate of the campervan was now open and Phyllis could see that there was a heavy duty mobility scooter tucked right behind the rear seat.

"Is that for you?" Phyllis asked Mrs Grant.

"Yes, I'm determined to still get out and about as much as possible so we've just bought this campervan. We had it especially converted to get my scooter in. I'm Sally and my husband is Garry. Come and have a look inside."

Sally climbed in to the camper van and sat on the front seat, now swivelled round to face into the van. She told Phyllis that she had Multiple Sclerosis, having been diagnosed three years ago. Prior to that, she and Garry had loved their mountain walking but sadly she was no longer able to do that so instead, to provide access to the outdoors, she now had a mobility scooter.

"It's got fairly large wheels so we can still get out along quieter roads, disused railway lines, forest paths etc. We've even managed to get it up a trail almost 1500 feet above Loch Ness!" Sally explained. "I'm thinking of writing a book based on the places we've been which are suitable for scooters, wheelchairs or buggies. I can still walk but not very far."

Phyllis was impressed by her positive attitude and was pleased to tell her that Camus now had a disabled washroom if that would be of any help. It was obvious however that Garry was preparing to erect the awning so Phyllis agreed to return later to show them around the site. She was touched by her new guests and was determined that their stay at Camus would be memorable. Little did she know that the Grants would certainly have occasion to enjoy every minute.

During the afternoon, the local minister called by to invite the church party to the regular service set for 11am on the Sunday, giving them an opportunity to meet the regular congregation and stay to share tea and coffee. It was a nice gesture and the group were more than happy to accept her invitation. They were planning to have a BBQ that evening, to which the minister and her family were invited. There would be a few humorous games and a quiz for everyone to enjoy. Whilst the minister was there, it was also suggested that perhaps the locals would like to accompany them on a final walk before they were due to leave on Tuesday. The minister told them that sadly she had a funeral arranged on the Monday and that most of the congregation would be attending but perhaps some of the locals would take them on a tour after the church service, on the Sunday afternoon.

The next arrivals were a smartly dressed couple who appeared to be in their sixties. They booked in as Mr Stuart and Mrs Hart from Wales, Phyllis noticed that they had different surnames but she had learned, through the years, not to ask awkward questions. Very often, during the visitors' stay, she would put the pieces of the jigsaw together and reach her own conclusions. She would often try to tell Reg what she had surmised but he rarely listened. After almost 40 years of marriage he knew that she got a lot of pleasure from her imaginative mind.

When Reg appeared to show them the site, he introduced Mr Stuart, whom he had now learned was called Ted, to Fergal. There was obviously a shared interest as Ted had restored an old classic car many years ago. It was his pride and joy much as Fergal was to Reg. Ted had taken the car to several shows and won awards. It was an Austin 7 type 65 which meant nothing to Reg but Ted told him that he had a series of photos of the restoration which he would love to show him. Once he started on the subject, he went into the technical details of parts and how he sourced them. Clearly he could stay and talk for hours but Reg politely told him that he had other guests to attend to and assured him that he would come back and look at the photos later. Mrs Hart, now introduced as Gwen, looked bored stiff as Ted had clearly trapped another victim. She had heard it all hundreds of times before! They both seemed pleased with the site and especially when they found that there were no children around. Reg informed them that the children were now back at school but that they often had families during the school holidays. Ted and Gwen didn't have children and they clearly had quite an aversion.

"We hate it when balls are sent flying past our windows" said Ted. "People don't seem to control their children these days."

Reg said nothing. He loved it when Camus was alive with the sound of excited kids running around and was really looking forward to seeing their grandchildren in just a few weeks' time.

Sunday afternoon saw the church party donning their walking boots and coats and setting off to follow the locals on a guided tour. It was a fine day but a few clouds were menacingly passing overhead. One of those days when you could be lucky and stay dry but best that they go well prepared! The group had met many of the locals at church in the morning and now seemed quite comfortable in each other's company as they headed off across Norman's field towards Angus's house.

Norman was in his field proudly gazing over the fence at his ladies and his calf, now almost 3 weeks old. Angus had given the calf a Gaelic name, as was traditional for Highland cattle; he would be called Gilleasbuig or Archie in English. His mother was Caitin meaning Willow Blossom. Archie was a feisty calf, full of spirit and was clearly showing the signs of being curious about all the visiting guests. Perhaps he would take after his father in patrolling the humped-back bridge. His youthful skips and jumps were carefully observed by his mother. His fluffy, curly coat made him appear as if he was begging to be cuddled but Reg and Phyllis had put a big notice on the reception door advising all visitors to take care. Although the Highlanders were generally a peaceful, placid breed, their maternal instincts are strong and it is therefore not advisable to get too close. Not that you could get too close to Archie, who was constantly on the move apart from when he was asleep, hidden deep in the long grass.

Three more calves were expected any time now and Angus was checking on the cows at least twice each day. Two had calved previously but the third was a heifer and this calf was to be her first. The expectant cows had been brought by Angus into the nearest field so that he could keep a constant eye on them. The Highlander breed normally calves quite easily and relatively quickly. Angus generally preferred to leave things be and experience had taught him to adopt a policy of minimal intervention, allowing a closer bond to develop between mother and calf. He had called in to the office that morning to say that from the look of their udders two of the cows were due in the next few days and the heifer was imminent. Phyllis was quite excited and asked Angus whether she could help to choose one of the names when they arrived.

"Of course you can hen" said Angus "but you'll have to follow my suggestions and you'd better improve your Gaelic!!"

Whilst Angus was still in the reception, Garry could be seen taking the mobility scooter from the back of the campervan.

"Look at this couple" said Phyllis watching from her window. "The lady has got Multiple Sclerosis so she has to use a scooter. It's so sad to see young folk so affected don't you think Angus?"

"There's a lady in the village who's got MS" Angus replied "She's got a boy in the same class as Paige but she doesn't let it stop her from doing anything. Makes you feel lucky to still be fit doesn't it?"

"Where do you think she would be able to go on that scooter" asked Phyllis "You know all the little tracks round here."

"Well she can obviously stick to the road and probably make it to the ferry but off-road would probably be more difficult. I think that there are a few good paths in the forest on Niall's estate but I haven't been there for ages" replied Angus.

"I'll suggest it to her." said Phyllis. "She's planning to write a book about places suitable for people with scooters or wheelchairs. I'd like to help her if I can."

Garry and Sally made their way to the road and turned down to the humped-back bridge. Being an experienced outdoor couple, they had sensibly strapped an umbrella to the back of the scooter seat and Garry had a full back pack; no doubt they were also equipped with full wet weather gear. The pair were laughing and smiling all the time. They both had a set of binoculars and stopped from time to time to look at the variety of birds flitting between the trees. Sally had learned to love the scenery and the wildlife when they used to enjoy their mountain walks. Although they couldn't continue that passion, they could still explore together and, armed with their binoculars and a camera, they could share in the infinite delights that nature could offer.

"Just look at the burn. Isn't it beautiful?" remarked Sally. "Oh and look at the siskins. I wish that we could see them back home; apparently they are around at the country park but I've never spotted any, have you?"

The birds were darting across the burn as it flowed underneath the bridge, revealing the bright yellow streaks on their wings. The burn was no longer in full spate, just a steady flow of crystal clear water lapping over the stones, continually submerging the plants as they struggled desperately to return to the surface. The sun's rays were piercing through the leaves above, sparkling on the water and showcasing the colours of the numerous flowers littering the sides of the burn. Higher up the bank the tight buds of the foxgloves would be likely to burst into their purple or white splendour in a month or two's time. The invasive rhododendron bushes were also preparing for the summer; they would bloom in May or June, adding their pink hue across the landscape.

"Did you know that there are now various projects along the West Coast to clear these bushes? Garry asked his wife, pointing to the rhododendrons "They may be spectacular but apparently they cause a great deal of damage to the native species".

"Yes, I know" replied Sally "but I still love the explosion of colour that they provide in many of my photos".

Garry and Sally always took their camera with them, ready to capture any opportunity nature might offer. On this short outing they had seen a woodpecker high up in the trees and animal prints in the mud at the side of the burn. Their progress was purposefully slow as they continued along the road and were eventually out of sight.

While they were out another smart caravan pulled onto the site. It was a Swift Challenger with its distinctive panoramic front roof window. Phyllis was delighted as her friends Mick and Maureen approached the reception. She immediately put the kettle on, enticing them to stay and catch up. They had bought the new van at the start of this season. Now that they had both retired early they had decided to treat themselves and planned to spend much of their time touring around. Reg had seen them arrive and made his way across the site to the reception to welcome them. They had exchanged Christmas cards ever since their first visit. In fact Phyllis now sent over 60 cards to former guests with a few notable exceptions. She always included a note about the various improvements they had made to Camus and assured them all that a return visit would be most welcome.

"We were inspired, all those years ago, by Pat and Paul's van. Do you remember it?" Maureen asked Phyllis.

Phyllis tried hard to think back to their first season but was clearly struggling "To be honest I can't" she replied.

"Don't you remember the posh couple with everything colour co-ordinated" prompted Mick.

"Oh yes" said Reg "they had smart green wellies and folding bikes which looked as if they were never used".

"We've stayed in touch ever since" said Maureen "but I don't think that they've been back to Camus."

"I've got to find out - are you still painting Maureen?" Phyllis felt compelled to ask.

"Yes, but I'm not getting any better" replied Maureen modestly.

"Well then I've got something to talk to you about later" said Phyllis "Go and get yourselves set up first then we can catch up some more".

Phyllis was glad that Reg and Mick had wandered towards the door and therefore didn't hear her talk to Maureen about her painting. She was hoping to keep her plans a secret.

Their friends set off across the site and once again chose a pitch looking out to sea. They parked up next to Garry and Sally's outfit, having improved their awning erection skills since they were last at Camus. This time the awning went up without the quarrels that were evident last time. It was clear that Mick was watching the clouds passing by, conscious that it could start to rain at any minute. A drop of rain would probably be quite welcomed by Mick. It would give him an ideal opportunity to get out his chamois and wipe the traces of mud from his brand new van!

Sally and Garry returned a little later in the afternoon. Although there had been a threat of rain, they had managed to escape and return dry. They immediately struck up a conversation with their new neighbours. Phyllis was watching from her window. It was an ideal opportunity to venture out. Garry and Sally might like to see the steading and surely Mick and Maureen would be impressed.

As Phyllis approached the party they all turned to say hello. Sally got off the scooter and Phyllis could now see that her gait was clearly affected. From Phyllis's manner it soon became obvious that Mick and Maureen had been to Camus before but through their conversation it emerged that Garry and Sally were hardly strangers to the area either.

"I was wondering whether you would all like to come and see the steading which Reg has converted?" asked Phyllis.

They all said that they would but Garry was particularly keen. He was very interested in history and as they walked across the site it became obvious that he knew a lot about the area and the highland clearances.

"Will you be able to make it across the camping field?" Phyllis asked Sally.

"Yes, I think so. It's not far and it does me good to walk" Sally replied, taking Garry's arm for support. On the way she staggered and occasionally stumbled, all the time laughing at her own plight. The others politely slowed down whilst Garry kept a strong hold ensuring that she could make it all the way. En route, Sally explained to the others that she had multiple sclerosis but that it had done nothing to dampen her enthusiasm for Scotland and the beauty it has to offer. Clearly everyone in the group had that in common.

Inside the steading, the guests were complimentary about the conversion Reg had undertaken and Phyllis was proud to mention the contribution made by her son, Ryan.

Garry's previous job had been a property services manager so he was paying particular attention to every detail. Both Maureen and Sally loved the tartan cushions and asked about the impressive photo of the barn owl. They sat round the table and the conversation led from one topic to another.

"We always come to The Highlands. We don't ever think about anywhere else." Garry announced proudly.

He continued to list the places in Scotland they had visited and offered lots of recommendations. Mick and Maureen mentioned their previous trip to Ulva which Garry picked up on with real knowledge and interest, revealing that his great-grandmother came from Ulva and that he had researched much about the island and its history.

"You must come over to our van one evening and have a drink. We'd love to hear more about it" said Mick, directing his invitation to Garry and Sally.

We'd love to" replied Garry "We've got loads of pictures and I've got a book all about the island,"

"Before you all head off, I'll ask Reg to make sure that you can see Fergal while you are staying here" said Phyllis. "Fergal is the old tractor that Reg has restored. He's really proud of it. Oh and by the way Maureen I've got a favour to ask you".

Phyllis quietly took Maureen to one side. "Would you have time to paint Fergal while you're here? It's our ruby wedding anniversary on 2nd June and I'd love to give the picture to Reg as a present. I'll pay you of course".

"It will be a pleasure" replied Maureen with a beaming smile.

As the party left the steading, they met Ted and Gwen. Ted could hear Mick and Garry talking about the old tractor which gave him a cue to join in. Whilst Sally and Maureen returned to their vans, Ted manoeuvred the conversation to his beloved Austin 7. He told both Mick and Garry that he had brought with him lots of photos of his restoration and would make sure that he showed them before they all moved on. Of course people are happy to share experiences whilst on caravan sites but neither of the men looked overjoyed at the prospect. Mick and Garry had really hit it off well. They both had a great sense of humour and Mick had an infectious laugh which made everybody smile. It was to be the start of a real friendship which was to grow as the week progressed.

As promised, they shared a delightful evening together in Garry's van. The banter and humour were obviously enjoyed by everyone. Sally and Maureen also had a lot in common, especially when Sally revealed that since she had MS she had started to sketch the scenery. Maureen showed her a few of the pictures she had painted and gave Sally useful tips for a novice.

"Garry has just taken up fishing so while he's off with his rod I thought that I could sit and sketch. I'll show you one I did last year" Sally said, reaching up to one of the overhead cupboards. "I'm not very good at it yet but I find it very relaxing. I'm only using pastels at the moment but I'd like to progress to paints. Is painting messy Maureen?"

"No not really, once you get yourself set up. It's probably no messier than pastels. Have you seen my painting of Phyllis's baskets hanging in the reception?" Maureen proudly threw in to the conversation.

It was one of those awkward moments when Sally would have loved to say yes but she couldn't. She would be sure to check it out though next time she was buying some rolls. Garry was very good at filling those difficult silences so he, in turn, stretched up to the cupboards and pulled out his book 'Sin Mar A Bha' or 'Sheen Mar a Var' as he phonetically pronounced the Gaelic.

"If you enjoyed your visit to Ulva you'll love this book" said Garry proudly. It means The Way It Was and it's all about the island.

"So tell us again, what is your connection with Ulva?" asked Mick

"My great-grandmother came from the island. She died when I was 10 but spoke so fondly of her beautiful island. Apparently she used to walk about on the island with no shoes on. You know what it's like when you're 10. I was never really that interested in the stories she told me but since then I've done a lot of research and we've been to Ulva several times" explained Garry. "Now that we've been there, I just wish I could talk to her again. I've got so many questions I'd like to ask her now".

"We first went there before I had MS and we walked to Ormaig" Sally continued "Did you go to Ormaig and see the old ruined crofts?"

"Yes we did" replied Maureen, now riveted with interest.

"Did you see plaque explaining that the Ormaig was the seat of the MacQuarries?" Garry pitched in. "Well my great-grandmother's name was Jessie MacQuarrie."

Both Mick and Maureen were captivated by their stories and the lengths Garry had gone to researching his family history. They heard how Garry had first visited the island wearing his kilt in the MacQuarrie tartan, instantly recognised by Donald the ferry man, and how some Belgian tourists had asked to take a photo of Garry standing by one of the old tumbled down houses. He now had a real desire to walk a fair way across the island to Cuilinish, where his great-great grandfather came from. Of course Cuilinish was no longer there, only sparse ruins. The trouble was that Sally couldn't possibly get there now; although the scooter was off-road it wouldn't be able to cope with the bumpy terrain nor get across on the small passenger ferry. Also Cuilinish was a good two hour walk, each way, from the ferry.

Garry had, for several years, said that he'd love to find Cuilinish but that he wouldn't go without Sally. Sally had been researching on the internet before they started this holiday to see whether there was anybody on Ulva who could help. She had found the name of a man on the neighbouring island of Gometra and had contacted him.

Iain, who was the shepherd on Gometra, agreed to take Sally and Garry by boat around the island of Ulva to reach Cuilinish. Garry was really looking forward to it. He knew that most people would question his desire to get there but he was not deterred and the trip was planned for the coming Wednesday.

As the week went on, both Mick and Garry were very conscious that Ted was waiting to pounce. He would sit in his van, reading through his classic car magazines and watching their every move from his window. Garry made sure that he was always busy, usually on the way out with the mobility scooter, embarking on yet another excursion. Ted was a nice man but he was a fanatic. Finally catching Mick's attention one morning, he took half an hour to show his photos and explain all the technical details of his restoration project. Each day Garry would laugh that once again he had escaped. On the Wednesday morning Ted was up early and was pleased to see that Garry was out of his van without the scooter. He quickly called across.

"Morning Garry, have you got time today for me to show you my pictures?" he asked.

"Oh I'm really sorry but we're off to the ferry in a minute and we'll probably be gone all day. Have to catch up with you some other time" replied Garry in the knowledge that, once again, he had managed to avoid the inevitable. He just couldn't wait to tell Mick.

Although Iain had planned to take them to Cuilinish by boat, the wind had picked up considerably overnight and when they had woken up in the morning the gales were obviously too strong. Garry was devastated. The trip would surely be cancelled, but Iain contacted him by phone to say that he had come up with an alternative plan.

"Meet me at The Boathouse and I'll take you in my sheep trailer on the back of the quad bike!" suggested Iain, quite matter of fact.

They all met at the Ulva Ferry Boathouse. When Iain arrived he had thoughtfully strapped a plastic garden chair, using typical 'farmers' orange string, into the trailer for Sally to sit on.

"I thought that your wife might need a chair, it's a fair way" Iain said to Garry.

"Great Iain, she'll be fine on that" was Garry's response.

Off they went, with Garry stood up in the trailer like an ancient Roman gladiator in his chariot and Sally hanging onto the chair for grim death. There are no roads on Ulva, just farm tracks with rocks, divots and mud and the trip to Cuilinish took about an hour of almost uninterrupted bumps. The plastic chair was consequently shunted around the mucky trailer but it was all part of the adventure. Sally had a permanent grin on her face all day.

It was great that Iain could take Garry right to the ruined village of Cuilinish. On the way they had passed so many settlements, all cleared in years gone by. Sally was particularly saddened by the sheer number of ruins and the vision of so many people who would once have lived there. Without Iain, Garry would have found it impossible to identify Cuilinish from all the other tumbled down buildings but once they arrived Iain allowed him some quiet time to trek through the bracken and ferns to reach the remains of the buildings, some of which were a significant size. Garry spent a while searching amongst the stones hoping to find some evidence of habitation, He would have loved to find maybe an old tool or implement but sadly he found nothing. He was deeply moved by the experience though. Cuilinish was the place that his great-great-grandfather had come from. He could picture the days when these buildings were real homes, with women cooking and children playing. He even imagined that he could still hear the now silent voices. After the clearances his great-great-grandfather was forcibly moved to the Gorbals in Glasgow. What a shock this must have been, to be torn from such beauty.

They returned via the same bumpy track. On the way back, Iain seemed to assume the role of a tourist guide, stopping periodically to point out places of interest, for example 'Starvation Row'. The name itself profoundly describes the ruined row of cottages with no roofs, the original thatch having been deliberately burned away to evict the helpless, superfluous tenants, thereby 'Clearing' the land to make way for the lucrative production of sheep. When they finally returned to The Boathouse Café, they met up with the skipper of Turus Mara whom they knew from a previous trip to Lunga. He had been unable to take out his boat due to the strong winds. There was considerable banter between them all. Iain had revealed during the long bumpy ride that he was also the shepherd on the small island of Eorsa, which was always referred to on the Turus Mara trips as famous for 'absolutely nothing'! Sally revealed, with great pleasure, that Eorsa was indeed famous for something: sheep! They finished off their memorable day in the Café enjoying a wonderful bowl of home-made soup and bread, followed by scrumptious cake and piping hot coffee.

Garry could not get over the kindness of Iain. Taking people across the island was not usual for him. The trouble he had gone to in preparing his trailer with a chair was certainly appreciated. The whole experience had fulfilled a long awaited ambition for Garry and was certainly something which both he and Sally would, forever treasure in their hearts.

# PUFFINS AT LAST

Although Reg was not known as a romantic, he was totally aware that this year would see their 40th wedding anniversary but he made no mention of it to Phyllis. He would be sure to get a card though next time that he was in the village. They didn't usually exchange anniversary presents but Reg had an idea, one that he planned to explore when he got the chance to have a quiet word with Angus.

When Angus arrived the very next morning he had more news to share. The heifer had calved, it was a girl and both mother and baby were doing well. She was a happy little calf, almost golden in colour. Angus had chosen several names but Phyllis could make the final choice. He had written his shortlist on a scrap of paper which he left in the reception for Phyllis to consider. The names on the list were:-

Sonaseg meaning Little Happy Female
A Bhuidhe Ailidh meaning Yellow Beauty
Neonag meaning Daisy
Faoilte meaning Delight

Or

Niseag meaning Little Ness

They all sounded wonderful but Phyllis still struggled with the pronunciation. She particularly liked Niseag as it reminded her of Ellie's fascination with the Loch Ness monster. Having been advised that Niseag is phonetically pronounced 'Nish- ack', she warmed to her choice even more. She made two coffees which Angus carried away from the reception. He found Reg in his workshop as expected.

"Mornin auld boy" was Angus's usual, friendly greeting.

"Hi Angus" Reg replied "Got any news?"

"Aye, I've got another calf and she's a fine one too" said Angus with a smile on his weathered face.

"Have you got a minute to chat" asked Reg.

"Aye of course. Come and have your coffee" said Angus dragging across one of the stools which Reg kept by his bench.

The pair sat down. Angus was keen to hear what Reg had on his mind. It was usually his latest project, something he was planning to make. Reg started off slowly, reminding Angus that Annie was making her plans to move to Scotland. He told his friend that he was beginning to feel that it was time for him and Phyllis to find a permanent home near Camus. There was no longer any need for them to return to Worcester during the winter months but they would need something better than their caravan in which to spend the harsh winter. Angus knew that there were only a handful of properties nearby, none of which were currently up for sale, but when Reg started to ask Angus about building a new house it became clear what was on his mind. He had extended the lease of the site with Hamish, Angus's father, but only for three years. Would Hamish consider selling some land to him? Angus was more than just a bit excited and said he would certainly talk to Hamish. The conversation went on with Angus explaining how he had secured planning permission for his own house and how long it took him to build it himself. He was getting more involved than Reg was expecting.

"Don't breath a word to Phyllis or Elaine though" Reg asked "It's just an idea I've got and I want to check it out before we go any further."

The two men stayed in the workshop for ages. They both liked the thought that they could plot and scheme, sharing a common secret. When Angus took the empty mugs back to Phyllis she commented that they had been in the workshop for ages but Angus said nothing, making out that he was telling Reg all about his calf and looking at Reg's current project.

That evening as Phyllis turned the page on her calendar she got yet another twinge of excitement. Annie and the family would be here soon. She just had to pick up the phone and check the latest news.

"Hi Mum how are you?" came the response.

"We're good and looking forward to seeing you all. Do you know what day you are coming?" asked Phyllis.

"Yes, we're starting in Stirling on the 26th May and we've booked in to Meg's on the 29th. We're going to pick up some house details and may go back to look at a few while we're at Meg's. Will you and Dad be able to look after Ellie for a while so that we can go house hunting?" asked Annie who had clearly been working it all out.

"What about William? We could have him too" Phyllis responded not thinking what it would take to look after a toddler still less than a year old.

"No, its ok we'll take him with us but Ellie would love to spend some time at Camus. Oh and by the way we've got a surprise for you. I can't say what it is but make sure you keep May 31st free." Annie's voice was clearly bursting with excitement.

Phyllis was struggling to think what was being arranged but she knew that if she were to ask Reg his response would be that it wouldn't be possible for them to leave the site unattended as they had many bookings for the holiday week.

"We'll be here of course on the 31st looking after the site. What are you thinking of?" Phyllis's mind was already whizzing. Perhaps they were planning a BBQ or something as it was her anniversary on 2nd June.

"I'm not telling and don't ask Ellie, she's sworn to secrecy" continued Annie.

They continued chatting for ages about the houses they had seen on the internet. With the money Annie and Craig were likely to get for their house in Worcester they might be able to afford a house with either four or five bedrooms near Stirling. The estate agent had been round to see their house and had been very positive about selling it. Annie was hoping that if they could find something, when they came at Whitsun, they might be able to move in during the school summer holidays, which would be ideal.

"So what have you got planned for 31st?" Phyllis asked again hoping to catch Annie off guard.

"I'm not saying Mum just wait and see. Anyway must go now and check what William is up to - it's gone a bit quiet in the other room!"

The following morning Sally appeared in the reception and told Phyllis all about the trip to Cuilinish. Phyllis laughed when she heard about the mucky sheep trailer and was so pleased to hear that they had enjoyed a fantastic experience and also fulfilled Garry's ambition. She was pleased to report to Sally that Angus had suggested some suitable tracks for her scooter on Niall's estate and immediately offered to show her a map of how to get there. After getting directions from Phyllis, Sally bought a few more rolls for a picnic and returned to her van to plan the outing with her husband. Both Garry and Mick were out with their chamois, cleaning their vans. It seemed that the two men had more than their sense of humour in common. Fortunately Ted and Gwen had left early to go to Fort William so there was no chance of a boring half hour looking at photos of Ted's 'classic' Austin.

Part of Niall's estate was forested and Phyllis's directions took them to a car park right by the main entrance to the forest. Garry lifted the mobility scooter from its designated spot in the back of the camper van and they were soon on their way through a heavy wooden gate. It was a nice dry day, in fact the rain had stayed away for several days now so the ground was quite firm. The path was softened by layers of conifer needles which also rendered their movements quiet, not likely to scare away the birds and animals that they were hoping to see. They had always considered themselves lucky with wildlife having previously seen dolphins, a basking shark, both the golden and the white-tailed sea eagle, otters, deer and a huge variety of smaller birds but they were still wanted to spot a pine marten; maybe today they might be lucky again. Garry was convinced that in order to see these animals you needed to be out there, not simply looking from a car window, and you needed to know where to look. This conifer forest might well contain pine martens and red squirrels so they had their binoculars ready.

The route through the forest was ideal, fairly flat and firm but occasionally blocked by a fallen tree or branch. It was usually possible for Garry to move such debris but on one occasion they had to divert off the track and around through the fallen leaves getting stuck in the softer ground below.

"Oops, can you hang on a bit" Sally called to her husband "I think I'm stuck!"

Once again her dilemma made Sally burst into laughter but a bit of manhandling by Garry and further giggling from Sally soon saw them on their way again. In a few places, previous heavy rain had left muddy sections to cross. The large wheels on the scooter coped quite well but Sally made notes that it would be harder for smaller scooters or wheelchairs to follow this route. The forest was popular with cyclists and Sally simply added to the numerous tracks made previously by others.

Occasionally they would come to a clearing where shafts of bright sunlight would pierce through, revealing the strands of spiders' webs linking the trees and bushes together. Encouraged by the light, the forest floor would rise with mounds of moss as if in celebration. Fallen branches were being consumed by lichens of green, yellow and silver, creeping steadily and adding a variety of colour to the thick carpet. It was a welcome relief from the dark brown hues which dominated the wood.

Their route took them to a huge nest of wood ants near the edge of the forest. It captured their attention by the constant activity of the thousands of ants coming and going with determined purpose. Sadly it reminded them of London in the rush hour with hoards of commuters speeding across bridges and down narrow alleys. The nest was a dome shape, built with pine needles all carefully collected and carried by teams of workers, many still bringing new material to the nest. Sally wondered how they each knew what to do and who was giving the orders. The nest must have been almost a metre high, a considerable structure for such tiny creatures. Garry made a small indent using a stick picked up from the forest floor. The ants reacted instantly, seeming to draw in reinforcements to attend to the damage. He was only trying to observe the activity and soon the ants decided to move on.

As they reached the end of the path, the route took a sharp turn left, leading out of the trees and giving a clear view down to the heather-clad valley below. The sunlight here was uninterrupted; the pink rhododendrons were beginning to open and were simply glorious. It was a perfect place to stop for a picnic. Time also for Sally to make notes in her book about the route they had followed and its suitability for other disabled visitors. As well as the state of the paths, Sally carefully recorded what there was to see, how far they had gone and how long it had taken. They had been out for over an hour and she noted that the views from this clearing were particularly inspiring. For lunch they had cheese rolls and piping hot soup which had been heated on the double burner in their camper and carefully put in to thermos flasks.

While they were eating they could hear the grouse feeding in the heather and the piercing screech of a buzzard, soaring high up above them. Using their binoculars they watched it disappear into the wispy clouds emerging a short distance away but still circling over its trusted patch. There were no pine martens to report yet but they had seen a few red squirrels hastily bounding across the paths within the forest.

"I doubt that we will see any pine martens in the middle of the day. I think that they become more active at night" said Garry.

"You never know" Sally replied "We've always been lucky before."

After lunch they continued on the path, which skirted the forest before meeting a small burn where there was a purpose made wooden bridge, keeping them out of the water trickling slowly below. They could see the hoof prints of deer leading down to the water showing that they had clearly been there but as it was now almost midday they knew that they would be unlikely to see them. If it were the evening they might be luckier but previous experience had taught them that this was not a good time. They continued on the path for another hour, eventually taking them back through the forest to the wooden gate from where they had started.

It was on the way back that Sally had a truly unique experience. Making her way steadily on her scooter through the trees and past a jagged rocky outcrop, something flew straight towards her. It was quick but smaller than a bird.

And before she could prepare herself for the impact it landed on her leg. Looking down to see what it was, she was amazed to see that it was a tiny, cute bat. From the wildlife programmes she had seen on TV she thought that it was probably a pipistrelle. It was smaller than a mouse, no bigger than the size of a matchbox. It had landed on her trousers, looking up so that she could clearly see its face.

"Garry quick come over here" Sally whispered, beckoning Garry to come and see but not wanting to call out for fear that the tiny bat would take off again. "Why do you think that it's landed on me? Do you think that it's injured?" she asked.

Garry came over and studied the cute animal. He had never seen a bat so closely and considering how adept bats are at avoiding impact and seeing that there was no obvious sign of injury he could only assume that it was young and inexperienced. The creature was clearly reluctant to leave. Eventually Garry moved it onto grass hoping that it would take off again and come to no harm. Up until then Sally's scooter had no name but from that point on it was to be known as The Batmobile!!

When they finally returned to their camper they had still not seen any pine martens, although they were sure to be there. Once back at Camus, Sally made her way to the reception to thank Phyllis for her recommendation and relay her bat report!

"That was a really good suggestion. Thank you. I'll certainly be adding that to my list" said Sally.

"So what did you see?" asked Phyllis.

"We were hoping to see a pine marten" Sally replied "but we know how hard they are to spot".

"You should ask my friend Meg at the B&B down the road. She regularly gets pine martens on her bird table and she really wouldn't mind. Just tell her I sent you. You've probably passed her house, its called Taigh Meg" said Phyllis.

Sally returned to her caravan and noticed that there were now several more vans on the site. The new arrivals were busy setting themselves up and erecting their awnings. She greeted everyone with the usual hello and was met with a similar friendly response. She and Maureen had taken the prime views but there was still plenty of space looking out to the sea. There was certainly no feeling of overcrowding at Camus. As she got close to her van she could see Garry setting himself up for a BBQ. He did love his home-made BBQ. None of those disposable trays for him! He was in his element when the BBQ was alight and had even been known to stand out in the rain under an umbrella whilst everyone else retreated sensibly into their vans. This evening was looking like it would stay dry. It had certainly been good weather since Easter and was looking good for the week ahead. Sally and Garry always came to Scotland prepared for the worst but more often than not they had experienced pretty good weather and this year even their trip to Ulva had stayed dry.

For the caravanners, the week seemed to pass too quickly but for Phyllis she was simply counting the days. When it was Garry and Sally's time to move on they came to say goodbye but not before Ted had made sure that Garry had seen his photos. Garry was actually in the process of taking down their awning when Ted strolled across to catch him. It was hardly a good moment. Garry had a well-oiled routine placing the poles out of the way and wiping the dew from the now hanging awning but he paid Ted's pride and joy suitable attention whist making it clear that he needed to press on. Sally came into the reception to thank Phyllis once again for a wonderful stay. They had seen so much and enjoyed every minute, especially Garry's trip to Cuilinish. It had certainly been a memorable week.

Maureen had been busy painting a wonderful picture of Fergal with its immaculate grey paintwork and pillar box red seat. She had made a sketch quickly whilst Reg had taken the tractor from his workshop and then she completed the landscape backdrop separately before adding Fergal. When it was time for them to leave she invited Phyllis to her van to see what she thought.

"I hope you like it" Maureen said "I painted the scenery and then added the tractor afterwards but I'd had to take the detail from a sketch I made before Reg put it back in the workshop".

Maureen had captured the light so beautifully giving a real sparkle to the paintwork. Her picture showed Fergal on the beach with a mill pond sea behind and the subtle darkened image of islands in the distance. Fergal was clearly the star but Maureen had incorporated the colours of the beach, the rocks, the kelp and the sea so perfectly.

"I absolutely love it" said Phyllis with real sincerity in her voice. "It certainly does it justice, in fact I think that it makes it look better than it really is but I won't tell Reg that. I'll bring my car over and put it in the boot. I'm going to Meg's later so I'll keep it there."

And so their good friends Mick and Maureen went on their way again promising that they would not leave it so long before their next visit.

As the rhyme says, the April showers had certainly encouraged the May flowers. The buttercups and celandine both brought a carpet of yellow across much of Camus whilst down near the shoreline sea plantain was emerging from the rocks. The calves were happy in their field skipping and playing with each other, occasionally chasing the crows as if to assert their authority. Phyllis couldn't wait for Ellie to meet Niseag and, of course, Archie. She was looking forward to having her granddaughter whilst Annie, Craig and William were away in Stirling. Meg was also preparing for their arrival and had made up several stories about the calves which she was keeping in her head for Ellie and William.

May carried on as usual with yet more caravans and campers. The weather was good for Donnie's kayak business and several visitors commented on the experience in Phyllis's visitor book. Reg's new woodpecker bird box was definitely occupied judging by the constant visits being made by both parents. Through binoculars it was clear that the box was in use by a pair of green woodpeckers. Reg had heard the intense bouts of rhythmic drumming earlier in April. He had appreciated the skills employed by the birds in perfecting the opening which he had started. They had green plumage and a distinct red head. It was quite rare for them to be seen so far west, which made Reg feel rather privileged.

The morning of the 29th of May arrived at last. Reg and Phyllis were up early making a start to their daily routine. Meg was expecting Annie, Craig and the children in the afternoon and was busy changing the beds and baking a welcoming tray of scones. They finally arrived at 3pm, only stopping briefly to drop off their suitcases before making their way to Camus. Meg would prepare their favourite stovies for the grown ups' evening meal whilst Phyllis would feed the children at tea time. Ellie was very excited and this was clearly rubbing off on William who was trying desperately to take his first steps before being unceremoniously flattened by his sister, who was skipping around pretending to be a highland calf. After a quick stop for Meg's tea and scones, the family were secured in their vehicle for the final short trip to Nanny and Granddad.

Norman was waiting by the bridge, a sort of informal welcoming party. Ellie wound down her window to call to him but William was too small to see what was going on and started to cry.

"Hey, don't start that now. Nanny won't want to hear that silly noise" said Annie turning in her seat.

"There's Norman" squealed Ellie "He's come to see us."

Phyllis had already opened the gate having been tipped off by Meg. Both she and Reg were waiting to greet them.

"At last" said Phyllis as Ellie ran and jumped straight in to her arms.

"And where's my little boy then" said Reg as he leaned in to the car and went to get William from his car seat.

William was startled and immediately started to cry again.

"Here let me get him out" said Craig "he'll be ok in a moment. How are you both?"

"We're fine and really pleased to see you all" said Reg. "Come to the van and we'll put the kettle on".

Ellie stepped momentarily into the van but then ran straight back out wanting Phyllis to show her the calves. Phyllis would have loved to stay and spend time talking to Annie but she could hardly ignore her granddaughter's pleas so she left the others in the van and took Ellie's hand. William loved the van as he could comfortably hold on to all the cushions and make his way around. If he fell down he could quickly crawl around and would soon find something else to grip hold of. He had soon stopped crying and was standing up, holding on to granddad's trousers.

Annie was fairly excited. Before she and Craig had left Stirling they had been to see a lovely farmhouse on the outskirts of the town. They needed to check out the schools but they might well go back in the week and look at it again. They had looked at several new-builds but they wanted a reasonable garden for the children to play in and that mainly came with older properties.

Outside, Phyllis and Ellie had made their way to the field in which the calves, Archie and Niseag were playing. There were now, in total, four calves all cute and cuddly but Phyllis made sure that Ellie understood that she was not to go into the field on her own. She didn't want to frighten Ellie but explained that the mummies were very protective of their new babies. Perhaps Angus would take her nearer when he called in. Returning to their van, Phyllis got out some paper and colouring pencils which she had bought. Ellie sat down quietly, making a drawing of Niseag and allowing the adults to catch up. William was quite content playing with the coloured plastic pegs which he had pulled out from one of the cupboards.

Annie was still struggling to keep the secret of her plans for the 31st but as it was now only two days away, she needed to spill the beans.

"You know how you've always wanted to see the puffins mum?" asked Annie "Well we've arranged for you, Dad and Ellie to go to the Isle of Lunga on Wednesday".

Both Reg and Phyllis were initially quiet. Who would look after Camus? How should they react without upsetting everybody? Before they replied Ellie fortunately broke the silence.

"It will be really exciting" she said "We will go on a boat and take a picnic. I'll help to make it".

"Before either of you say anything, it's all worked out" continued Annie "Meg and I will look after the guests, Craig will empty the bins and Donnie will take care of the campers. Meg knows all about it and I've already booked Jimmy's ferry for the three of you. So what do you think?"

Reg and Phyllis were speechless. They really hadn't expected this and were not accustomed to having a day off. As the idea sunk in they admitted what a lovely surprise it was going to be.

"I'll need to show you a few things" Reg said to Craig.

"We'll come back later and sort everything out when the children are in bed. Meg's going to bath them and read some bedtime stories. She's really looking forward to it" said Annie.

"Perhaps Reg would hold the fort and I can come with you to put the children to bed" replied Phyllis somewhat jealous that Meg was lined up for bath time. "There's some

left over casserole in the fridge you could have" she told Reg
"You won't mind if I go with the children will you?"

Reg took the children down to the shore while Phyllis
made them some tea and Craig went with him, leaving the
ladies in the van to catch up. William was excited by the
water, wriggling in his dad's arms in an attempt to break
free. Craig let him splash at the water's edge, soon resulting
in William having soaking wet trousers and slimy marks
on his new t-shirt but he clearly loved the experience, one
which he would grow to enjoy over many years Reg hoped.

Annie, Craig, Reg and Phyllis stayed for a while catching
up on the details of Craig's new job and the houses in Stirling
that they had seen so far. Reg was nervous about leaving the
site and their guests for a whole day. He spent ages telling
Craig what might have to be done during the day and how
to deal with any emergencies that might arise. Of course
most of these details had been meticulously documented by
Reg and were unlikely to occur; after all, they would only
be away from about 8am to 6pm and Donnie was always at
hand to help. Just in case, Reg thought that he would ask
Angus to call by and check up. Phyllis showed Annie the
visitor registration form which would need to be completed
should any new guests arrive. Based on the bookings they
had taken, two caravans were expected on the Wednesday
but there was no indication of the time they might arrive.
She gave Annie a brief introduction to the till and the daily
bread deliveries which should arrive by about 8.30am.

By Wednesday Phyllis was intensely excited about the trip. She always loved hearing about the puffins from her guests but now, at last, she was going to get the chance to go herself and to take Ellie along was a real bonus. They started on Jimmy's ferry with a few other Camus guests who were taking the same trip so there were plenty of people to chat to which, of course, Phyllis revelled in. Reg took Ellie to the bridge where she helped to steer the ship towards Mull. They then transferred to a smaller boat taking them to the Ulva ferry from where they would catch the final boat operated by Turus Mara, taking them first to Staffa and then on to Lunga. Reg was still worrying. His head kept racing back to Camus and whether Craig would be able to cope. Although he had taken his mobile, Phyllis was insistent that he should not use it but instead he should enjoy this rare day off. She had a large rucksack filled with sandwiches, cakes, crisps, sweets and drinks which would see them all through the day. Ellie had already asked for the crisps and they hadn't reached dry land yet.

The final boat to The Treshnish Isles was wonderful. She was named 'Hoy Lass' and was ready and waiting for them at Ulva ferry. Phyllis had heard so much about Ulva but sadly there wasn't time today to take the short passenger crossing to the island. Looking across to Ulva, the sea was a wonderful blue. They were so lucky with the weather and Phyllis hoped that it would last. As the boat sped away the plumes of white spray soared behind. It felt like they were going really fast but in spite of the sun there was a distinct nip in the air and Phyllis made sure that Ellie put on her hat and gloves to keep warm. The crew drew their attention to points of interest along the way and Ellie had her binoculars round her neck, all the time telling Phyllis what she could see.

The boat did have a small toilet which Ellie had to visit of course, partly through natural curiosity but also probably due to the excitement of the day. Phyllis took her hand and made her way to the lower deck. Negotiating the steps was quite tricky though as the boat bounced and swayed. It seemed determined to tip them over which made Ellie giggle especially when her grandmother finally lost balance and plonked on to an empty chair.

They soon arrived at the Isle of Staffa with its formidable basalt columns rising proudly from the sea. The waves were crashing into Fingal's Cave with its pillars as tall as a cathedral. Of course Ellie did not recognise the famous music played by the skipper and seemed relatively unimpressed as Phyllis tried to tell her about the famous composer Mendelssohn. She was keeping a look out for puffins through her binoculars but hadn't seen any yet. As the boat moored up to the jetty, Phyllis told Reg that she didn't really want to take Ellie along the jagged, cliff-edge path to the cavern. Instead she and her granddaughter would climb up the steep steps to the grass above and anyway Ellie was ready for her sandwiches. Reg did go however and was truly impressed by the scale of the cavern. He followed the others along the crude walkway just above the high water level. The cavern echoed with the sound of the swelling sea and waves rushing in. Reg had seen many sights around the world during his years in the army but there was something particularly memorable about this natural wonder. Within the cavern walls, Reg was at last relaxing, no longer thinking about Camus; he could almost relate to the feelings which must have inspired Mendelssohn. As he joined Phyllis and Ellie back at the top, all three enjoyed their picnic still wrapped tightly in their scarves and jackets. The views were simply stunning but the wind was blowing, threatening to sweep away any loose wrappers. It was obviously a day for photos and Reg took several, especially when Phyllis and Ellie were framed against such a wonderful backdrop. He looked back down to the boat waiting patiently below, bobbing about as if it were urging them to get back on. When the crew were indicating to them that it was time to move on, Reg and Phyllis collected their things and carefully made their way back down the steps with Reg going first in case they should fall.

The boat sped on to Lunga, once aptly referred to as 'a green jewel in a peacock sea'. Ellie was becoming increasingly excited as the island came into view and especially when she caught sight of her first puffin bobbing about on the water.

"Look nanny, there's one" she cried out, pointing ahead.

Phyllis looked through her binoculars and felt a twinge of excitement in her stomach. She had seen so many photos and heard so much from all their visitors but now she was here. She could hardly believe it. She had wondered whether it would be an anti-climax after all these years but it was certainly not that. They made their way across the rocks which Ellie managed with ease. Reg offered his arm to give Phyllis support as she slowly picked her way over the unstable rocks, carefully following the well trodden path towards the ascent.

"Come on nanny!" called out Ellie, pointing up to the cliff, "there's more puffins up there".

Phyllis dared not avert her gaze from her feet lest she stumbled and fell. Oh what it would be like to be youthful again although, in her heart, she was certainly feeling the same excitement as Ellie.

"Thank you dear" she said to Reg as they reached the path taking them to the grass beyond. "You go on with Ellie and keep her away from the edge. I'll be fine now".

As they made their way higher up to Lunga's lush green grass, Reg spotted some old ruins which he was keen to explore. Ellie and Phyllis had already seen some of the many puffins which were abundant along the cliff edges. They were keen to get closer but continuing further would ensure that they could pick a choice spot.

"You carry on and take a look around" Phyllis said to Reg "I'll stay with Ellie and we'll find a good place to sit".

Phyllis couldn't believe how close she was able to get to the puffins. Ellie was old enough and sensible enough to stay away from the edge. Initially she rushed excitedly to get nearer to the birds but when her Nan encouraged her to sit quietly she soon realised that it worked just as well. They chose a spot a few feet from a burrow from where they could hear the curious sound coming from below. Phyllis encouraged her granddaughter to put her ear to the ground and listen. Ellie did as she was told and soon heard a sound which she tried to repeat, urging her Nan to do the same.

"No it goes like this" said Ellie making a noise from the back of her throat as if she were surprised by something.

Phyllis tried to do her own version but it wasn't very good and made Ellie burst into laughter. Another puffin came up, from below the cliff edge, landing only a few feet away, stopping to take a careful look at them before moving towards the burrow. What a comedian, with its bright, colourful beak, black eyes and white face. Phyllis was mesmerised and felt that she could stay there forever. Annie had certainly planned a lovely treat. Ellie was keen to check out the other puffins all landing and taking off from the cliff edge. Some birds had set up burrows a little bit further inland. In fact wherever Phyllis turned she could see puffins in all directions. In one spot Phyllis could see both puffins and rabbits in neighbouring burrows seeming quite happy in each other's company.

"Do you want some cake?" asked Phyllis.

"No thanks Nan. Can I go up there?" the little girl replied. Ellie was simply too excited to stop and eat.

When Reg returned to join them he was happy to finish off the sandwiches they had started on Staffa. Now sitting quietly, he took out his camera again. The puffins presented endless opportunities for photos. Reg caught several in flight and some with nesting material in their beaks. Whilst Ellie wasn't aware he caught numerous photos of her with puffins all around. It was great to capture those natural moments when Ellie wasn't looking. If she knew that a photo was imminent she would pose like some superstar with a false smile. Appealing though it was, it would take away the wonder of the moment.

Phyllis was sitting peacefully, thoroughly enjoying every moment. She reflected for a moment at the nice gesture engineered by Annie. They would not have ventured on this trip were it not for her suggestion and planning. Both she and Reg had finally been given the opportunity to enjoy the puffins, just as so many of their guests had done before. Although the puffins were clearly the highlight for Phyllis and Ellie, the boat trip and the wonder of Staffa had made a lasting impression on Reg.

Before it came time to leave and board 'Hoy Lass', Reg asked Ellie if she would be able to take an anniversary photo of her nanny and granddad. She was a sensible little girl and well able to cope with granddad's point and click camera. The happy couple sat together on the grass, surrounded by puffins, with the sea as a stunning backdrop. Ellie got a little carried away with her important task taking a number of photos. When she passed the camera back to her granddad, Reg could see that a few of the images were a little skewed but there were several worthy of the photo album.

On the return journey they snuggled up together, sandwiching Ellie between them to keep warm. Phyllis even suspected that Reg had briefly nodded off, a sure sign that he had truly relaxed. He was always a hard worker and it must have done him good to have at least one day off. Her own thoughts returned to Annie and how nice it was going to be when they moved to Scotland. These family occasions would be easier now and she was really looking forward to watching the children grow. In a few years' time they could maybe go again with William, assuming that they were still at Camus of course. Right now Phyllis couldn't ever imagine wanting to move away. She loved this west coast with its unpredictable sea, the captivating wildlife and the welcoming nature of the people which drew you in as if held in a warm embrace.

Puffins on Lunga

Meet the neighbours

Hoy Lass 'Turus Mara'

Cuilinish

Equipped for adventure

The beauty of the landscape

Basalt Columns Staffa

Taking after Norman!

Iona Abbey

Iona with a turquoise sea

The courtyard Iona Abbey

Stacked limpet shells

Ready for a deer fence

The Boathouse Ulva Ferry

*Jessie MacQuarrie*

View from Ben Nevis summit

# HOME IS WHERE THE HEART IS

Upon returning to Camus, Annie and Craig were pleased to report that everything was in order although Reg couldn't resist making his own sneaky inspection. Ellie was excitedly telling her mum every detail about their trip, making it difficult for Phyllis to get a word in edgeways. At first Phyllis didn't notice that William was no where to be seen.

"So where's William?" she asked Annie.

"He's gone back to Elaine's" Annie replied "They came to check that we were ok and Elaine wanted him to go back to her house. Apparently Camran and Paige were asking to look after him so I've had quite a lazy day. I must ask you Mum, have you all had a good time?"

"I simply can't begin to tell you" Phyllis replied with tears in her eyes. "Thank you so much. I didn't just enjoy it, I loved every moment and I know that your dad and I will remember it forever."

The vans had arrived during the day as expected and Annie had completed the registration forms, with Donnie showing the new guests around the site when he returned from his kayaking, so there was nothing left to be done. Reg and Phyllis wanted to go and introduce themselves to the new arrivals so, as soon as Reg returned from his inspection; they walked across to the two vans. The first family, the Blunts, had two girls aged five and seven and the other family, the Warrens, had two boys of six and eight. Ellie immediately made friends with the children. She was keen to show off her knowledge of the best places to play and so they ran off to check the shore.

"Elaine is asking us to leave the kids with her tomorrow while we go and see a few houses. We thought that we might stay at a hotel overnight. What do you think Mum? Meg says she will put the kids to bed on Thursday night and I was hoping that you and Dad might have them during the day on Friday – I know that it is your anniversary but we'd be back by late afternoon". Annie was waiting to judge the response.

"Well I'd have to pick them up early on Friday so that Meg can look after her B&B guests. We'll manage won't we Reg" said Phyllis, feeling that it would be a nice way to repay Annie for the trip to the puffins but also a privilege to spend time with the grandchildren before they returned to Worcester.

"I think that you should stay overnight at Meg's with the children. It's not fair to leave it to Meg when she's got to be up early for breakfast" Reg chipped in.

With the children occupied, Phyllis, Reg, Craig and Annie retreated to the van for an eagerly awaited cup of tea. It gave Reg the opportunity to run his latest idea past the family.

"I've been thinking, how would you feel about selling our bungalow and moving up here permanently?" Reg asked Phyllis completely out of the blue. He was not known to embellish or dramatise things.

Phyllis was taken by surprise. Reg had never indicated to her that he was ready for such a big step. After an uncharacteristically brief silence, Phyllis lent across the caravan to give Reg a big, embarrassing hug.

"I'd really love it Reg" she squealed with childish excitement. "I don't feel I belong in Worcester anymore especially now that Annie and the family won't be there. What have you got in mind?"

"Well, I've been talking to Angus" Reg continued "He thinks that I should speak to Hamish about the lease of the site and also about the possibility of buying some land, but I wanted to ask you first".

"I think that would be great" said Annie, grasping Craig's hand "You both love it here but where exactly would you live?" she asked her Dad.

"I'm not sure yet but if you think it's a good idea I'll take it further" Reg announced to the now captivated family. "Don't tell anybody though; I've got lots to think through."

Soon Elaine was back with William, Camran and Paige and the older children ran off in search of Ellie. Elaine could sense that there was a feeling of real excitement around but she put it down to their wonderful trip. Angus had been true to his word and had kept his conversation with Reg quiet. Having previously agreed that she would have both the children again the next morning, Elaine confirmed that she would bring them back to Phyllis in the afternoon.

By early evening, Annie, Craig and the children had returned to Meg's. When it was time for bedtime stories, Ellie insisted that Meg told her a story all about puffins and it didn't take her long to fall sound asleep.

The following day went as planned with the children spending the morning at Elaine's, after which Phyllis was in her element with both of them all afternoon, taking sheer delight in watching William having fun crawling around. Fortunately it had not rained for quite a while so he was dirty but not muddy. Phyllis took them both for a walk, with William in his buggy. She just had to take them to see Joyce and was hoping that she might see other friends along the way. Ellie was collecting wild flowers from the hedgerow which she would make into a bouquet for Meg when they returned there to sleep. She never stopped talking, asking questions about the caravans, the puffins, the kayaks and her move to Stirling.

"Mummy is so excited about a new house. I'll be able to see you more often won't I Nanny?" she said as she skipped along.

"Yes you will" replied Phyllis "You can come and help me when you're on school holidays."

"Can we go to the bridge to see if Norman's there? William would love to see him too, wouldn't you William?" Ellie asked.

Obviously William didn't answer; he was too busy waving the long feathered grass which Ellie had given him.

Arriving at The Ferry Boathouse, Joyce hugged Ellie again and also begged Phyllis for a cuddle of William. This was the first time Joyce had seen him as he hadn't gone on the boat trip the previous day. She pulled up a highchair for William and took Ellie to choose a cake.

"So tell me all about your trip to the puffins yesterday. Was it good?" Joyce directed her question at Ellie "Jimmy isn't back with his boat yet otherwise he'd take you on board" she said to William.

Phyllis went into every detail of their boat trip - Staffa, Lunga and of course the puffins. Once she got started there was usually no stopping her but William unknowingly had his own agenda. Having enjoyed his juice and chocolate biscuit he was anxious to get out of the highchair and started to whinge. Phyllis was going to have to get used to these interruptions. As she lifted him out, it became clear that he needed to be changed so Phyllis took him and his essential bag to the toilet. Ellie meanwhile went around the counter to help Joyce serve the next customers.

Eventually they returned to their caravan for tea. Granddad sat quietly with the children reading stories while Phyllis prepared some boiled eggs with soldiers just as she used to do for Annie and Ryan. She simply loved having the family close again and was experiencing a real feeling of contentment. After their tea she took them back to Meg's and could hardly wait for her own sleepover with her good friend. First it was bath time and then time for stories but Phyllis was particularly pleased that Ellie wanted a story from her Nan even though Meg had earned an enviable reputation. It seemed strange that Phyllis was spending the night at Meg's. She should probably be thinking about poor old Reg, on his own in the caravan but she was far too busy telling Meg all about their day out and her thoughts about moving permanently to Camus. She was rabbiting on so much that her voice became more and more strained. It was obviously time for bed. She remembered to collect the picture from Meg and put it in to her car for the next day.

It was now 2nd June and as soon as she and the children returned to Camus, Phyllis went to her van, placing the wrapped picture carefully on the table. Reg was on his rounds emptying the bins but he was soon back to meet them.

"I've got something for you" she said to Reg giving him a peck on the cheek "Happy anniversary."

Reg carefully opened the parcel "My god it's Fergal. What a beautiful painting. Where did you get it?" he asked full of emotion.

Phyllis told him that the picture was painted by Maureen who had sketched the tractor when Reg had left it on view. He loved the colours of the backdrop and how smart Fergal looked. For now he would hang it in the reception, replacing Maureen's previous picture of the baskets. When they moved to a house this picture would surely take pride of place.

The season was advancing quickly and the start of June saw Annie return to Worcester having made enquiries about the fixed price farmhouse. Fixed price properties were becoming a welcome feature to those moving from England, taking away the uncertainty of placing an offer over the asking price and hoping that the offer would be sufficient. They had engaged a solicitor in Stirling recommended by Craig's new employer and things were starting to progress.

Reg also was keen to move things on, having made arrangements with Angus to call by and see Hamish. Leaving Phyllis at the reception, he called at Hamish's house to find out what options might be possible for buying some land and possibly building a home for him and Phyllis. He picked up Angus en route to interpret Hamish's strong local dialect.

Reg had not been to Hamish's house before. They had been in his company several times at Elaine's and sometimes at Meg's but never before at his small cottage. Reg was surprised at his humble dwelling, an old, single storey cottage, freshly painted white by Angus. The pretty little garden, waiting to burst into colour, was Hamish's pride and joy and down the side was an immaculately tended allotment for his vegetables. The whole area was fiercely protected by tall wire fences erected to keep out any raiding deer. Angus explained that his father had lived in that cottage all his life. Angus himself had grown up there sharing a bedroom with his two sisters and his elder brother. Hamish continued to remain in the cottage even after losing his wife and when Angus built his own house he offered to build a purpose made annex for his father but the cottage held many fond memories and Hamish was comfortable there.

They went inside to the small living room which was simply furnished with two old armchairs, a wooden table, an old fashioned stove and a deep sink. On the dresser was a radio and in the corner a TV. The TV was the only modern appliance around, probably because Hamish was forced to go digital in recent years.

"Hello Reg" Hamish said "How are you laddie and how's Phyllis? I'll put the kettle on."

The men started the conversation with the usual news about the caravan site, how many lobsters Angus had caught the day before and an update on the new calves. The subject then moved on to Reg's thoughts about moving to Camus permanently. Hamish identified immediately with Reg and Phyllis's love of the land. He had far more land than Angus needed for his sheep and cattle and remembered back to the days when he rented out the land to other local crofters but the demand was not there anymore. He also spoke so fondly about his wife, Angus's mum.

"She was a beautiful lassie" he said his eyes filling up. "We had a good life on the croft, hard but good. Her name was Jirvel - it means true desire".

Angus explained that Jirvel (Jir-vel) was the proper pronunciation of the Gaelic word Dearbhail or Dorothy in English.

"She used to sing in the fields while we gathered in the hay. Do you remember that Angus?"

"Aye I can still hear her now" replied Angus resting his arm on Hamish's shoulder in comfort.

"So Angus has told me that you want to build a house here. What exactly have you got in mind?" Hamish asked Reg.

Reg felt a little uncomfortable and had been hoping that Angus might follow up on their earlier conversations but Angus was leaving it to Reg.

"Well, I was thinking that it is about time that I looked to buy the Camus site if you're prepared to sell it. Did you hear that we've just been upgraded by the Tourist Board?" Reg asked.

"Aye son and you've done well. Your visitors have brought so much to the area. The shops are busier and Donnie is doing fine too. Ye canny stay in that caravan much longer though," Hamish replied, leading to the next obvious question.

"I know" started Reg "I was wondering whether you had another bit of land where I could build a house for Phyllis?"

Hamish thought that was a good idea but said that he and Angus would be best placed to talk that through. First he would have to de-croft some of the land. Angus knew all about that as he had de-crofted a plot for his own house. Hamish and Angus knew the local planners and the workings of the Highland Council so they would start to make enquiries. Hamish knew that Reg would get a lot of support from the locals. They were always talking about him whenever he made his way to the village each week, on his quad bike, to buy his regular paper 'The Oban and West Highland Times'.

Having received a favourable response from Hamish, Reg was left to continue his plans with Angus. They hadn't spoken about money yet but Phyllis still had money left to her by her late father Henry and they had only used a small amount when converting the steading; also their Worcestershire bungalow would easily fetch £300,000. Angus would get his surveyor to look at the croft and suggest a suitable site for a property, taking into account the drainage and the soil. Reg would need to have a conversation with Phyllis regarding the plans but he also needed to set the ball rolling with regard to selling their old bungalow.

Back at Camus, the Blunts and the Warrens were having a great time. The children seemed quite happy playing on the caravan site with occasional trips out. Both families went to the lighthouse and the Warren boys loved taking their bicycles into the forest, returning splattered with mud as boys do. All the children wanted to have a go in the kayaks but at least three of them were too young so in fairness they all had to miss out. The girls were keen on horses so the Blunts took them to the nearby stables for a ride. They were taken around the local bridleways on a lead reign by two stable girls. Mrs Blunt walked alongside them but as the girls were still young a half hour ride was quite sufficient. The stables had about a dozen Highland ponies in a variety of colours. The eldest sister, Megan, was on a mouse-coloured pony while her younger sibling, Jess, rode a cream one. They seemed quite big and stocky for two tiny girls but Highland ponies are renowned for their quiet temperament and were perfectly suited to young riders. As they walked, the stable girls told Mrs Blunt that Highland ponies had a long history in Scotland. In days gone by they were used on the crofts for ploughing and there were still a few kept on the estate. Some are still used during the stalking season for transporting deer carcases, on special saddles. They are strong and well able to carry a large stag down the mountain sides.

The bridleways were alive with birds making frequent visits to their nests to feed their hungry chicks. The girls loved the ride, sitting with their hands gripping the front of the saddle or pommel. Their legs were placed in the stirrups although Jess's hardly extended beyond the saddle flaps.

The weather at Camus was holding out and visitor numbers were good. Geoffrey and Ronnie returned and Geoffrey was really pleased to see that his photo of the barn owl was now on display in the steading. Many new bookings had been made following the TV programme and Donnie had also had an increase in the number of campers including a booking for 16 school girls and two female teachers, so was planning ahead for the school party arriving in a week's time. The teacher had sent him a letter explaining that the holiday was particularly focusing on PSHE. It stood for Personal, Social, Health and Education and the teacher was asking whether Donnie could suggest some activities which would encourage teamwork to improve the girls' physical skills and give them the opportunity to exercise and eat healthily.

He sat down with Reg and e-mailed a reply to the teacher. They could offer kayaking, team games - possibly clay pigeon shooting, if the school thought it appropriate - and obviously wildlife spotting. The area was famous for seafood and Donnie could arrange for them to have lunch at The Ferry Boathouse but he would need to give Joyce fair notice. If the weather was good they could prepare their own burgers for a BBQ one evening. Reg and Phyllis were so pleased to hear that teenagers were getting the opportunity to explore the outdoors and were keen to give the girls a holiday to remember.

The girls arrived in two minibuses, typical 16 year old girls, all giggly and excitable. Reg took them all for a welcoming brief in the steading and introduced Donnie who normally helped with the camping side of Camus. Donnie's presence was adding real interest for all of the girls. He was young, extremely fit, in both senses of the word ('fit' to the younger generation often refers to physical attraction) and quite strong for his age. Both teachers reminded the girls to be quiet and listen whilst Reg adopted the authoritative tone he was more used to in the army.

"Your first job" Reg announced "will be to put up the tents and suitably prepare the area. Have any of you put up a tent before?"

There were a few sniggers erupting into a series of comments between the girls as chaos descended within the steading.

Reg tapped the table. "Settle down girls. Donnie and I will be here to help. First you need to form yourselves into four groups, one for each tent. Many of your activities this week will earn points for your tent so you need to choose your friends wisely."

This information was met with a barrage from the girls all busy calling out each other's names but one teacher rose to the occasion requesting silence. She was Miss George and she kindly suggested that both Reg and Donnie should take a break while they sorted out their groups.

The two men disappeared for a cup of coffee, happy to leave the excited girls with their teachers. They could tell that this was going to be a challenging week. Between them they decided that Reg would supervise the erection of tent numbers one and two and Donnie numbers three and four. The girls were fortunately unaware otherwise the nominations for tents three and four may well have been oversubscribed!

When they returned, all was quiet in the steading. The teachers had obviously worked hard to calm the girls down. They had settled into their four groups and Reg told them to get their tents from the minibuses. He announced that the girls themselves would need to put the tents up and that points would be awarded for preparation, stability and time taken, although Reg advised that it was better to erect a secure tent last than a wobbly one first. When he revealed that he would be supervising tents one and two and Donnie three and four there were secretive mutterings going round the room but he took no notice. Before they moved back outside, Reg asked the girls if they had midge repellent with them. It turned out that some had and some hadn't so he advised the teachers to take them to see Phyllis in the shop. Before they rushed out Reg embarked on a biology lesson.

"Now then girls listen carefully" Reg started. "It's mid afternoon and the midges will be active at any time. A single midge is almost invisible to the human eye and you may be surprised to hear that it is particularly the female of the species which is vicious".

His statement was made with a certain sense of humour not shared by his audience. He continued;

"She requires blood and when she's alerted to your presence by smelling carbon dioxide in your breath she will attack - along with thousands of girlfriends!"

The girls, suitably alarmed, immediately headed off to the shop allowing Reg and Donnie to help lift their tents from the vehicles.

Erecting the tents was full of drama. Reg advised his teams that they should first find a suitable spot, checking the position in relation to the sun and the wind. They should then follow the instructions and familiarise themselves with all the equipment before feeding the poles through the appropriate sleeves in the flysheet. The tents need to be secured using the tent pegs and guy lines provided, using a mallet which Reg and Donnie had brought with them. Both he and Donnie would be on hand for advice if needed but otherwise they would observe from the side.

Donnie had adopted a less officious approach with his teams. The girls were anxious to get started but wondered if he could help them apply the midge repellent first. Miss George stepped in to rescue him telling the girls that, if they needed midge repellent, they were to ask her. The girls were particularly attentive to his every instruction, far more so than Reg's contingent.

It took a good hour for the girls to put the tents up with Donnie's teams seeming to require more help when it came to knocking the pegs in to the ground. One of Reg's tents collapsed during construction due to the poles not being firmly fixed. This sent the girls into fits of uncontrollable laughter while Reg flapped about trying hard not to take over. Eventually all the tents were secured. Now it was time for awarding points. They all scored highly for preparation with Donnie's teams doing better on stability and tent number one, Reg's, beating the rest on time. It was true that the midges had been attracted by the girls' activity so everyone retired to the steading for a cool drink and the batch of drop scones made by Meg. Following Reg's advice the girls were told to first make sure that their tents were zipped up at all times to keep the midges out.

Reg finally retreated to his workshop where he was assured some peace and quiet, leaving Donnie to sort out the itinerary for the week ahead. A BBQ was planned for the weekend when the local youngsters would join them; Kayaking was set up for the Tuesday and Thursday and clay pigeon shooting for the Wednesday. On Friday, Donnie had thought that they might catch Jimmy's ferry to Mull and visit Tobermory. On the way back they could eat at The

Boathouse and Donnie had a menu from which they could choose and place their orders in advance.

Miss George had sorted out a quick meal for the girls first evening. It was to be spaghetti Bolognese which she prepared on a camping gas stove in the mess tent. Each tent had to appoint one volunteer to help and to prepare the table. After dinner they would need to plan their meals for the rest of the week and Phyllis was asked for her advice as she knew the local suppliers, what was available and what it might cost.

They awoke early the following morning. The rota for showers had been worked out but the girls were asked to be mindful of other guests wanting to use the facilities. The whole process therefore took some time although Phyllis, knowing that there were no disabled guests on site, had kindly given them a key for the new washroom to ease the burden. Plugs and sockets for hair dryers and straighteners were not abundant so Miss George took great pleasure in teaching them how to look their best without these modern inventions. Before lunch they would go to the village to get their provisions and later Miss George had planned some orienteering. Each team was provided with a map and a compass requiring them to follow different routes all bringing them back to camp. The winning team would be the one which completed the task in the least time. Each team was allowed one mobile for emergency use only and a first aid kit which was to be carried at all times. Over lunch they planned their tactics and the noise from the mess tent was considerable - 16 girls with two teachers trying to keep order. Eventually they headed off and peace returned to Camus for a while.

Miss George had estimated that they would be back by 5pm and indeed the tent one team was home by 5.15. Others staggered back later with tent two last, due to taking a wrong turn at one of the given points and subsequently retracing their steps. There was considerable discussion regarding whose fault it was and there were a few humpy faces but this was soon interrupted by high pitched squealing coming from outside the mess tent. Tent two had obviously left the gate open and Norman was on the prowl. The sheer sight of his horns sent some of the girls in the direction of the steading whilst others simply watched from a distance.

"Look Miss it's a buffalo" shrieked Jodie.

"Don't be silly" said Miss George "It's a Highland cow. I saw it in the field earlier but I'm sure that it shouldn't be in here."

The sound of Donnie's voice could be heard approaching. "Hey Tormad, stop scaring the girls" he laughed. He had come to give them details for their kayak trip the following day.

Obviously undaunted, Donnie went right up to Norman and with a slap on the rear he headed him back to the gate but not before he had left yet another pat on the fresh grass just outside the mess tent. The girls still outside clapped and cheered but those inside were forced to step out gingerly, avoiding Norman's present. Donnie was full of apologies saying that he would be back shortly with a bucket.

Sixteen teenage girls on a kayak trip were a daunting prospect and Donnie's friend Rab had agreed to come, on both days, to help and support. The Tuesday morning induction session in the steading went well with the girls on a warning from Miss George that tent points would be deducted for disruptive behaviour. Rab brought his own kayak, so with Donnie's and the eight others they could accommodate two teams at a time, one supervised by Rab and the other by Donnie. The girls chose their craft, some preferring tandems, the others individual. The teachers also had a turn but when the initial splashing escalated to soaking, Miss George reminded the girls of her earlier warning. The morning included instruction and practice and trips around the bay. After lunch there would be a series of races with team points up for grabs. Things were set to become competitive!

The afternoon became serious with six races, each between two teams heading out to a buoy and racing back. Tandem kayaks with two people should surely have an advantage, so each tent was allowed only one tandem and two singles. However negotiating six craft round the buoy resulted in considerable bumping and clashing of paddles with bruises all round. Points were earned six for first, five for second and so on. Everyone loved it, especially when it was the turn for the adults. The two adult teams were made up of Donnie, Miss George and Bill, the coach driver, pitched against Rab, Miss Taylor and Gordon the other driver. The girls stood on the shore cheering and screaming with an obvious preference for Donnie's team, which was indeed victorious.

Earlier, while the girls were on the water, Reg had taken the two drivers to his shooting range as a forerunner to rough shooting which was booked for the Thursday. Reg quietly revelled in the compliments he received for his shots. The two men enjoyed it too and asked if they could join the girls for clay pigeon shooting on the Wednesday. Reg was pleased with the additional adult presence as he had not relished the thought of sixteen young girls armed with guns. True to form, Reg had however arranged with Donald in the village to supply him with four small guns with recoil-absorbing shoulder pads for the girls to use. Donald and his partner, Lewis, were coming to manage the traps and, along with Reg, to provide instruction. They were a rough-looking pair, with teeth missing and scraggy hair, but they had hearts of gold like many of the locals. They were always keen to take on a task if money was involved.

The shooting range was properly set up with all the necessary signage. Reg would have been sure to comply with all the necessary safety requirements. There was a Health and Safety risk assessment updated each season which he ran through with the teachers the previous evening but before the girls started he thought it necessary to give a full briefing in the mess tent. Points would be awarded for each clay successfully shot. Anyone being seen to depart from the instructions given would result in an instant dismissal for their entire tent. Reg did not mince his words. Surprisingly the event went according to plan with no incident. The girls enjoyed the challenge, a first time experience for them all. Assisted by Reg's encouraging support, tents one and two shot the most clays. There were however a considerable number of misses!

The Friday saw the girls looking forward to their trip to Tobermory and to the opportunity for some serious shopping, seeking gifts to take back home including Balamory souvenirs for younger siblings. Balamory was the famous children's TV show, filmed several years ago in this quaint colourful town. The girls enjoyed chips from the regular van on the pier, trying hard to fend off the persistent seagulls. There were also a few seals in Tobermory Harbour which were a rare treat, lovely to see and a memorable opportunity for holiday snaps. The teachers took them into the museum offering a selection of old photos and displays of life as it was many years ago. Although they had previously bought the food for the planned BBQ on the Saturday, they couldn't resist choosing some tempting cakes from the bakery with which to finish off the evening.

The girls had each contributed to a collection, intent on buying thank you gifts for the teachers, the drivers, Donnie,

Reg and Phyllis. For the teachers they bought some local hand-made soap, for Phyllis they found a delightful puffin ornament. They thought that it was particularly appropriate as Phyllis had told them so enthusiastically about the trip she had taken with her granddaughter recently. It took them ages to decide upon a gift for Donnie but they eventually chose a T-shirt with the word 'FIT' on it. Miss Taylor kindly agreed to take them to the distillery gift shop where she could buy three miniature bottles of Tobermory 10 year old single malt whisky. Of course the girls themselves were too young but Miss Taylor was getting on a bit at 25! The bottles were for the drivers and Reg.

They returned from Mull on Jimmy's ferry, complete with their purchases. Joyce had kindly prepared individual portions of cooked crab and some home-made coleslaw for them to take back and enjoy that evening.

On the Saturday evening, the winners of the tent competition were to be announced and the girls planned that they would give the gifts out then. They each took part in preparing the food and setting up the BBQ. Rab returned with a whole host of local teenagers and Donnie brought his CD player which was set up outside the steading. Under the watchful eye of Miss George, the girls were allowed to borrow a bowl from Phyllis and make up a fruit punch with wine, fruit juice and lots of lemonade. Phyllis and Reg had visited all the caravans to explain that it was the girls' last night and that a party was planned. They hoped that the noise would not disturb but nobody objected - in fact they were all welcome to join in as long as they brought their own food and drink.

Donnie had brought along some fresh fish for the BBQ, caught earlier by his own fair hand on Angus's boat. They all gathered round as Donnie skilfully gutted the fish, making his watching audience squirm. Once it was cooked, some of the girls simply couldn't bring themselves to eat it but those who tried it thought that it was delicious. There were numerous bones to pick out but it was still nice to try some truly local fresh produce.

The next day, still tired from the late night party, the girls packed up and squeezed their kit in to the minibuses. With hugs all round, especially for Donnie, they thanked their hosts and sadly said goodbye to Camus. Everyone agreed that a great time had been shared by all, one that they would always remember.

# WHEN IT RAINS
# IT RAINS!

Having enjoyed a prolonged spell of good weather, Reg and Phyllis had come to learn that it couldn't last. The rain finally came with a vengeance starting in June and continuing well into July. The west coast is known to be one of the wettest places in Europe, with annual rainfall averaging 180 inches, the mountainous topography forcing the warm, wet air, heated by the Gulf-Stream, to rise and form rain clouds. Not exactly what caravanners or campers want!

For days Phyllis watched from her reception window but there was little to see apart from guests hurrying from their vans to get their bread and milk or reluctantly making their way to the water points or bins. At times the rain lashed against the reception window, cascading down the pane, hiding everything from view, interspersed by brief respites as the dense clouds passed over and the sun would appear, returning light to the room. Phyllis hoped that it would soon pass but in the distance were yet more grey clouds, slowly moving towards Camus with their menacing load.

Reg was out in his wet weather gear emptying the bins and ensuring that the drainage channels were kept clear. Some pitches were awash with rain and several awnings had water lying under the groundsheets. Reg was more than happy to help the afflicted guests to move any drenched belongings off the ground onto tables, chairs or other higher positions. He had arranged for anything valuable to be moved into his store which provided secure shelter. Phyllis thought that he seemed a bit down, probably because several bookings had been cancelled.

Almost all of the campers had given up and moved to sites elsewhere, most likely further east, leaving the steading free for caravan guests to use. Phyllis decided to try something new to brighten everyone's mood. Back in Worcester, she and Reg had attended a few beetle drives in the village hall. Perhaps that would go down well at Camus or an evening of card games might prove of interest. There was also a game in the steading, 'Uno' which could be played by up to 10 people. Phyllis herself had enjoyed the card game 'Newmarket' as a child and there was always 'Rummy'. If her guests liked the idea she would prepare the beetle drawings. She knew that Reg was not a great fan but she felt sure that he would support her initiative.

Itching to leave the reception and engage her visitors in conversation, she put on her jacket and decided to brave it outside. There was no point in taking a brolly, not only was it raining hard but the wind was fierce, battering awnings and shaking caravans. She was offered a coffee in several of the vans and although she was not thirsty she accepted their kind offers giving her an excuse to stay and chat. The weather was the obvious topic of conversation and most appeared hopeful that she would bring news of improvement. Phyllis tried to reassure them that the rain would often pass quite quickly but they were not convinced. Initially her idea for a games evening was met with mixed reception. Couples were generally happy to keep themselves to themselves but, dampened by the weather, they were looking for something to lift their spirits and give them a chance to get out of their caravans. Phyllis used her powers of persuasion to assure them that it would be fun and encourage them to share stories. If they could bring their preferred drink, she would organise some nibbles.

When Reg returned to the reception, he found Phyllis deeply engrossed with paper and pen and struggling to draw the outline of a beetle.

"It's horrid out there isn't it" she said "shall I make you a cup of tea dear?"

"Yes please" replied Reg "what are you up to now?"

"I've just organised a beetle drive for tomorrow evening. Five couples - the Pecks, the Watts, the Webs, the Coopers and the Morgans - are all up for it" announced Phyllis.

"I hope that you haven't included me" said Reg with a dismissive tone.

"Well we'll need teams of four, so if we join in, that will make 12. I thought I'd organise something to cheer us all up. We used to go to the ones in the church hall in Worcester. Don't you remember?"

"Yes" sighed Reg. He only ever went to please Phyllis. Beetle drives were something he thought he had left way behind but he did admire Phyllis's enthusiasm and realised that it would, at least, give their guests a chance to socialise.

"I'm going to see Angus, if you're ok staying here. He's got some news about the house he wants to talk through" Reg told her "I'll be back soon."

"Fine dear" said Phyllis scarcely lifting her head from the pieces of paper "When you get back I'd like to pop to the village store to buy some nibbles."

Reg made his way to Angus's house just along the road from Camus, passing lush green fields along the way. The road was flooded in places and the burns were in spate having endured several weeks of rain. Even Norman was looking in a sad, bedraggled state as he lifted his head to watch Reg pass. Angus had heard from his surveyor regarding his thoughts on possible plots for the new house. Ideally they wanted to be close to the caravan site. The surveyor had explored a few different options. The first was to build on the site of the existing reception area incorporating a new purpose built reception/office. The drainage here was good and the connection to existing utilities was a plus, but although Reg delighted in the company of his guests he wasn't sure that he wanted to look out on them first thing each morning. Another possible plot was a little further on between Camus and Angus's house. It was one of Angus's fields currently used for grazing, mainly flat, finally tapering down to the water's edge. The views were incredible. A few established trees were hanging on, providing some protection from the wind; they had however, clearly suffered from the years of onslaught meted out by the westerly's, each tree listing characteristically eastwards like a row of giant meerkats nodding off in the morning sun. Reg wouldn't need the whole field, just enough for a house and a manageable garden. Utilities could be laid on without too much trouble therefore it was worth exploring. The third plot which Ewan, the surveyor, had investigated was just across the burn before reaching Camus. Once again it was currently used by Angus's cattle; an old byre with corrugated roof was still in use and would be ideal for Fergal. Again it was quite flat but ended at the cliff edge with no immediate access to the beach.

The two friends discussed the various options and agreed that Ewan should explore both fields further. Angus would make contact with The Crofting Commission regarding the change of use which would be needed before they could proceed further. He felt that he could make a strong case based on Reg's proven success with Camus and the increased tourist trade they had brought to the area. The locals were sure to support them. Angus suggested that Reg should use his architect, Alec, and was happy for Reg to borrow his house plans as a guide.

Reg returned to Camus and brought Phyllis up to date. Phyllis was becoming more excited by the day and agreed that, as soon as they had a dry evening, they would go and look at the two plots suggested. For now she headed off to the local store to see what she could buy by way of nibbles.

That evening the rain came down in stair rods. Inside their caravan the noise became quite intense, drowning out the television. They looked outside.

"Oh my god Reg look at the water" said Phyllis watching the puddles rapidly spread and merge together "the Coopers van is surrounded!"

Reg looked out. "I'm going to check the steading" he said. "This is the hardest rain we've had since we finished the work. I hope that the new roof is holding out." He put on his wet weather gear and made his way across the site.

When he arrived at the steading he found the Coopers and the Webs had taken refuge inside. Driven from their vans they were all sat around the table playing cards.

"Caught you practising for tomorrow" Reg laughed.

The couples were in good spirits "Well we didn't come here for the weather but we didn't expect this" remarked Mr Webb.

The steading was nice and dry, even cosy. Fortunately there was a basket full of dry logs which would be handy for the following evening.

"I'm afraid your van is now completely surrounded by water" announced Reg looking at Mr Cooper for a reaction.

"I know" came the reply "as long as it's gone in a few days cos' I've got to pack the awning away and move on."

"It will drain away quite quickly" Reg assured him "We had lovely weather earlier on this year. It's unusual for us to have so much rain. Surely it's got to stop soon".

The rain continued all the next day as the guests looked forward to the games evening. They met up in the steading at 7pm. Phyllis had laid out dishes full of crisps and peanuts and each couple brought along bottles of wine and beer. Reg started the evening by suggesting that they went round the table introducing themselves, where they came from and a little bit about themselves. He started off by telling the others how long he and Phyllis had been wardens, how they had developed the site and what they had planned for the future. By the time everyone had spoken it was already nearly 8pm but the introductions had set the scene and everyone was now ready for the beetle drive. Mr Webb stood out as a real character with a great sense of humour and soon had everybody laughing. They had several rounds of beetle drive whilst the rain continued to drum on the corrugated roof but for a while they forgot all about it, especially when Mr Webb began his repertoire of Tommy Cooper jokes, his party piece. He did a fantastic impersonation of the iconic comedian and had even brought with him a red fez which he pulled from a carrier bag in which it had been hidden.

"Heard the one about two aerials meeting on a roof, falling in love, and getting married? The ceremony was rubbish but the reception was brilliant" he started.

The others were all laughing which seemed to encourage Mr. Webb to continue.

"I went to the doctor the other day. I said 'have you got anything for wind' so he gave me a kite". This obviously prompted a series of doctor jokes.

"I went to the doctor. He said 'you've got a very serious illness'. I said 'I want a second opinion'. He said 'all right, you're ugly as well'."

Even Reg was crippled with laughter and was disappointed when Mr. Webb decided to remove the fez and with his gruff Tommy Cooper voice suggested that they should start a new game. They chose to play Newmarket in two groups of six, the ladies then the men.

Whilst the ladies played, Reg, by popular request, took the men to see Fergal. Typical men they were very interested in how Reg had completed the restoration and they loved the overall finish.

"Do you ever use it?" asked Mr. Morgan.

"Not really" replied Reg "I've taken him to the school fete in the village for the children to have a ride and he did appear in the TV programme I told you about but most of the time I keep him in here away from the elements".

As they returned outside and hurriedly made their way back to the steading, the rain appeared to be easing but the prolonged deluge had certainly left surface water covering many of the pitches. Reg was worried. He hadn't seen so much water covering the site before and feared that it might take considerable time to drain away.

The card games continued well into the evening. Everyone seemed to enjoy each other's company and they didn't return to their vans much before 11.30pm. A very successful evening they all agreed. Phyllis was naturally very pleased.

The next day Mr Cooper was out inspecting his now flooded awning. The rain had stopped and the sun was breaking through. By the afternoon the awning itself was fairly dry but the pitch was still a puddle a good few inches deep. They had hoped to move on the following morning so perhaps it would be a good idea if they could move to another drier pitch. Angus made his regular visit and was out with Reg, enjoying a cup of tea. Reg could see that Mr Cooper was surveying his predicament and the pair walked over to see if they could help. Mr Cooper asked Reg if he could change pitch to one less waterlogged.

"Yes of course" said Reg "You need to take your awning down though. Do you have some wellies?"

"No, not with me, I've only got my walking boots" replied Mr Cooper.

"I'll fetch some from my workshop" said Reg leaving Mr Cooper and Angus deep in conversation.

"That puddle is deep" said Angus "but you should be able to tow the caravan out slowly."

"Trust me to pick a pitch down here" laughed Mr. Cooper "I've got a bit of a slope to tackle!"

Reg returned with a spare pair of wellies and agreed to help Mr. Cooper to take his awning down.

"Do you want some extra help?" offered Angus. "It will be hard for you to keep it out of the puddle on your own."

So the three men set about the task with the enthusiasm of true boy scouts. Between them they managed to unzip the canvas and carry it away to higher ground leaving Mr. Cooper to sponge off the mud before packing it away. At the same time Angus left to go and check his creels. A little later Mr. Cooper backed his car up to the caravan. Hitching it up was a messy business, trying hard to keep the electrics out of the water. He got back into his car and started to pull forward but the ground was so wet that his wheels started to spin. The caravan wheels too must have sunk in to the submerged ground and it was proving difficult to make any progress. He tried to move forward slowly but with no success. Reg thought that he would get something to put under his wheels but in spite of his bringing some pieces of board from his shed, the caravan refused to budge. Mrs.

Cooper had sought refuge with Phyllis in the reception and together the ladies watched from the window. The other guests were now out making suggestions and watching the proceedings.

It was becoming obvious that Mr. Cooper's car was struggling with its traction. What was needed was a heavier vehicle with bigger wheels.

Reg had an idea. "What if we use Fergal!" he suggested with tentative enthusiasm. "I've never tried it before but it will probably work".

"I couldn't ask you to do that" Mr. Cooper responded "Fergal is your pride and joy!"

"Indeed he is" said Reg "but it will be good to see if he's got what it takes! Give me a minute and I'll bring him from the workshop". Reg turned excitedly, making his way to get his trusted friend. When Phyllis saw him make his way back on board his prized possession, she and Mrs. Cooper just had to make their way outside to join the watching crowd. Reg sat proudly on Fergal's bright red seat, bumping across the site, brimming with enthusiasm. At last the sun was shining and Fergal was gleaming against the stunning backdrop. The large wheels were flicking up mud leaving divots across the site but Reg didn't care. He was in his element manoeuvring Fergal close to the Cooper's van to rapturous applause from his audience.

"Don't celebrate yet" said Reg "we've still got to get it out!"

They hitched Fergal's tow bar to the caravan and after asking everybody to stand well back, Reg climbed back on board. He put Fergal into first gear and slowly moved forward. The caravan lurched slightly with a squelching sound as its wheels made their way from the puddle like the first spoonful of trifle being carefully extracted from its bowl. Fergal triumphantly continued onwards, taking the caravan to firmer ground, to the delight of the now cheering crowd. Reg finally settled on a pitch closer to the reception which would afford the Coopers an easier departure the following day.

Mr. Cooper gave Reg a hearty pat on the back as he climbed back down. "Well done Reg, or should I say Fergal"

Fergal was a bit mud splattered from his adventure but nothing that Reg couldn't clean up. Reg was quietly revelling in his heroic accomplishment. He wasn't going to put Fergal away in a hurry though as several of the guests were keen to take pictures of the 'dynamic duo'.

Phyllis laughed "I don't know which of you is the biggest star" she said referring to both Reg and Fergal. "Well done dear!"

They were now near to the end of July and Annie was due to move to her new farmhouse on 31st. She was on the phone to Phyllis practically every day, updating her on their progress. William was now one year old and Annie had held a birthday party for him and the other children he played with. Within the same week, Phyllis and Reg had accepted an offer for their Worcester bungalow and were now awaiting completion. Ryan was also due home from his tour of duty and had agreed to clear out the bungalow, placing anything they wanted to keep in storage pending their planned new build. He was then going to Stirling to spend time with his sister before coming to Camus for the rest of August, staying with Meg as he had done before. Phyllis was a little surprised that Ryan seemed to have such a long period of leave. He was spending time in Worcester then Stirling and told Meg that he would need a room without specifying for how long.

The summer finally arrived and so too did the visitors. Families came and both the caravan and camp sites were near to full every week. Weekly BBQs were organised for each Thursday with Donnie, Rab and Reg all helping out. More often than not, male campers took over the cooking. The meat came from the local butcher and it seemed to work well with visitors completing their requirements on a sheet pinned up in the steading which the butcher collected every Wednesday at lunchtime, delivering the produce to Camus each Thursday. The cost was set at £5 per person, enough to cover the food, charcoal and non-alcoholic drinks. It had even become a regular event for the local teenagers who were more than happy to join in.

With BBQs becoming so popular, it was often difficult to fit all the meat on the existing grills. Reg had therefore designed a new brick built structure which Ryan had offered to knock up when he arrived. It was to have a large griddle and a smaller one above to keep things warm. Reg had worked out the materials required and had made a tray to house the charcoal using metal from his workshop.

Phyllis was so excited when 31st July came and Annie and Craig finally moved in to their home in Stirling. Ellie was regularly on the phone to her Nan, telling her all about their garden and the new friends she had made with the children next door. She was looking forward to seeing her Uncle Ryan who was coming to help unpack her toys but with William walking properly now and in to everything, it was her job to keep an eye on him!

Reg and Phyllis were itching to visit Annie but the site was far too busy for that; it would have to wait. Besides which, Annie wanted to get settled before they invited visitors. It was great to speak to Ryan again without the awareness of distance; they worried constantly when he was on tour, Reg particularly, but he always tried to hide his feelings from Phyllis. Reg had been on many tours in hostile environments and knew only too well the price that some have paid.

Craig had been given two weeks leave from his new job to get settled in. The first week was spent helping Annie unpack all the boxes and Ryan's arrival was well timed. He could help move the heavy things around and was also a tremendous distraction for the children. For the second week, they had planned a surprise visit to see Reg and

Phyllis. Meg knew about it but was told to say nothing. When the two cars arrived unannounced at the gate, Phyllis was bowled over. She ran from the reception squealing with excitement and not knowing who to hug first. Ellie was the first as she ran and jumped at her Nan but Phyllis was longing to embrace Ryan. She hadn't seen him since he had left in March. Conscious of the dangers he faced when he was away, Phyllis always felt an overwhelming relief when he was home. Reg had heard the commotion even though he was, as usual, busying himself in his workshop. Seeing his family gathered outside the reception, he too felt a little overcome but proceeded to make his way towards them with his characteristic calm gait.

"What a lovely surprise" he said giving Ryan a firm, manly embrace "You didn't say you were coming."

"We thought we'd surprise you" said Annie.

Reg held out his arms to William who was happy to leave his dad and move on to Granddad but he was soon struggling to get down. Although Reg was keen to see him walk, the site was still muddy in places. The puddles were slowly disappearing but Reg knew that to William they would be a tempting distraction and he did not want a messy William to go into to his caravan. Ellie tugged at her Nan's arm, urging her to go and see the calves. She was wearing her flowery pink wellies which Annie had sensibly chosen. The guests could see all the commotion and guessed that the family had arrived. Several stopped Phyllis just to say hello to her beautiful granddaughter. Ellie was excited to see other children running around and playing. She peered through the fence to see the calves, Archie and Niseag, but they were a way off across the field and Ellie knew that she was not allowed in.

"They're much bigger now aren't they Nan?" Ellie said turning her attention to the other children racing round the site.

"You go off and play" replied Phyllis "I'll go back and make everyone a cup of tea".

William seemed to remember his previous visit to the caravan, going straight to the cupboard where the pegs were kept. Reg and Phyllis took real pleasure in watching him walk the short distance between the seats. Whilst they sat enjoying their tea, Annie told them all about her move and how much help Ryan had been. It was a bit crowded in the van so Reg lead Ryan and Craig out to talk about the bungalow in Worcester and Craig's new job. They hadn't gone far when they met one of the guests walking across the site, empty gas bottle in hand. He asked Reg whether he could buy a refill. Reg agreed to drop one off in a little while, taking both Ryan and Craig to his store where the bottles were held in a secure cage. Of course Reg had the appropriate key labelled up on his heavy bunch which he kept hanging from his belt.

"I'd better go back and check on Ellie. I'll leave you guys to it" said Craig as he headed back across the site.

"Here, come and see Fergal" said Reg as he told Ryan the story about towing Mr. Copper's van the other day.

The two men went inside the workshop where Fergal was duly cleaned up and looking immaculate.

"I've got something to tell you Dad" Ryan said with a hint of nervousness. "I've taken redundancy from the Army."

"Why?" asked Reg, somewhat surprised.

"They're cutting back on troop numbers so they asked for volunteers. I'm getting older now Dad and I want to settle down." Ryan continued, fully expecting to defend himself.

"What are you going to do instead?" asked Reg.

"I'm not sure yet" answered Ryan "but I wanted to tell you before Mum. Are you disappointed?"

"Not at all son" came Reg's unexpected response "You know that I've always worried about you even though I've never told you."

The two men chatted for ages about their army experiences and how Ryan would miss the camaraderie. He was now 30 and would like to meet someone, settle down and start a family. Spending time with Annie and the children had reinforced his feelings. He just hoped that he had not left it too late.

Ryan felt relieved that he had broken his news to his dad and although he had expected an adverse reaction, he had not received one. Reg seemed calm and Ryan was touched to hear that his dad had always worried about him. Now he just had to tell his mum. She would no doubt be overjoyed.

After a while, Reg and Ryan returned to the caravan to find everyone waiting for them inside. Annie, Craig and the children were due to return to Stirling the following day. They were only staying at Meg's for one night. Reg and Ryan agreed to stay at Camus so that Phyllis, Annie, Craig and the children could go back to Meg's for dinner. Reg didn't mind. He knew that, now Annie was closer, these visits would become more frequent and anyway he looked forward to spending quality time with his son. Before they headed off to Megs, Ryan took Phyllis outside to tell her his news. From the delighted cries outside, the family assumed that she was more than just pleased. She came back into the van wiping the tears from her eyes. Ellie thought that she had scarcely seen her Nan so excited and William picked up on the mood too, running the complete length of the van.

# IT'S ALL COMING TOGETHER!!

Phyllis thoroughly enjoyed the evening at Meg's, especially giving Ellie and William their bath. Annie let slip that she knew about Ryan leaving the army but had promised not to tell her parents as he wanted to break the news himself. Phyllis was on cloud nine. Not only were Annie and the grandchildren closer but now, hopefully, Ryan would be home too. With the Worcester bungalow about to be sold, it looked like Meg could have a permanent lodger! It didn't take much for Meg to suggest that they should open a celebratory bottle of wine.

Meanwhile Reg and Ryan enjoyed a true father and son evening talking about their lives and experiences. Reg knew that Ryan had a lot of adjusting to do to prepare himself for life outside the army. Perhaps it would be a good idea if he stayed around Camus for a while. Reg could vouch for the fact that it was certainly a peaceful place, good for the soul. Anyway, Reg could do with a hand, starting with the BBQ.

The next few weeks rolled on. The summer had truly arrived with warm sunny days and long evenings. Visitors came and went and Donnie certainly kept Ryan busy helping with the kayaks. Each Saturday evening, he and Ryan went to the Dobhran for a pint and Ryan soon got to know the locals.

There were a few memorable moments during the summer. One little boy broke his arm whilst scrambling about in the burn and an entire family fell prey to a severe reaction to midge bites resulting in swelling and irritation, but the worst story involved the Saunders.

The Saunders had an old caravan. They were not well off. They had only recently bought it so that they could enjoy more holidays with the children without too much cost. They were a pleasure to have on site and the children had a wonderful time.

Experienced caravanners will know that hitching up properly and double- checking becomes second nature. New caravans with their Alko stabiliser make it easier to see whether the van is firmly attached to the car but sometimes things don't go according to plan!

Mr Saunders had obviously thought that everything was fine as he wound down his window to wave goodbye to Phyllis in the reception. They made their way out down the narrow lane towards the bridge like so many others before. The bridge had a fair hump. The Saunders car went over but as the caravan heaved upwards, it became detached from the tow ball. The caravan rolled backwards with the awful sound of the A-frame scrapping the road. Fortunately they were not going fast but the caravan first rolled back then slowly forwards again, following the downhill slope towards the wall of the bridge. There was the horrible sound of crunching as the van smashed into the wall and the front corner took the full impact. Mr Saunders could see everything in his rear view mirror. It seemed that the whole nightmare was taking place in slow motion. Both the hump and the side of the bridge brought the van to an abrupt stop. Mr and Mrs Saunders jumped out to inspect the damage. The two children were kneeling up on the back seat to watch.

The impact with the wall had cracked the bodywork though not badly, nothing that a bit of strong tape would not resolve, but the electrics had been completely wrenched apart. One half was still attached to the car while the remaining broken cables lay forlorn and tattered along the road, hanging aimlessly from the van, which was now blocking the bridge and therefore also the exit and entrance to Camus. They had almost 300 miles to go. What would they do next? Whilst Mr Saunders looked helplessly at the severed cables, Mrs Saunders, thinking the worst, wished that they had paid for one of the recognised recovery services but before they left Mr Saunders had not signed up as it was an additional cost he could not afford.

"I'll go back to find Reg" said Mrs Saunders "You wait here with the children."

When Mrs Saunders returned to the reception, Phyllis was surprised to see her.

"Have you come back for something?" Phyllis asked.

Mrs Saunders looked harassed and sheepish "I'm afraid we've had an accident" she replied".

Before she could continue, Phyllis quickly asked "Is anybody hurt?"

"No, we're all ok but the van isn't. It came unhitched as we went to cross the bridge. Is Reg around?"

Phyllis knew that Reg had gone to clean the toilets so she hurriedly made her way to fetch him while Mrs Saunders asked if she could use the phone, which Phyllis duly moved towards her.

"Do you have the contact numbers for any of the recovery companies?" Mrs Saunders asked.

"Yes dear there's one on the notice board. It could have been worse though, at least everyone is ok" said Phyllis.

Mrs Saunders was panicking. She had no idea what to say but was anxious to find out what it might cost to get them all home and how they would pay for it. She dialled the number. The calm lady on the end of the phone clearly needed to know a lot more about the damage which Mrs Saunders was unable to adequately describe but when she pressed her about the likely cost of recovery she was told that to recover the van from Camus to Birmingham was likely to be in the region of £900. Why hadn't they taken out such insurance before their trip? Mrs Saunders ended the call saying that she would ring back. Her eyes were filling with tears when Reg and Phyllis re-appeared.

Reg put a reassuring arm around her shoulder "Let's go and see what's happened" he said "I'm sure it's not as bad as you think."

They made their way together down to the bridge: even Ryan offered to come and help. The children were out of the car standing quietly. Their dad was not in a good mood and they knew to keep out of his way. As Reg and Ryan descended towards the bridge, they could see the caravan listing into the wall, nose to the ground. Mr Saunders was surveying the frayed wires looking suitably embarrassed.

Reg immediately took charge and between them they managed to push the van off the bridge. Phyllis and Mrs Saunders took the children back to the site, passing Norman on the way. Norman had decided to make his way towards the bridge to see what all the fuss was about. Having checked out the commotion he decided to take the opportunity to graze the lush verge, further obstructing the proceedings.

It was not practical to push the van the short way back to Camus neither was it possible to get another vehicle past it to tow it out of the way. As Mr Saunders had initially thought, the damage to the old van was not too serious. Reg had some strong tape which he could use to make it safe and secure. Ryan turned his attention to the cables; fortunately he had experience with vehicle electrics. It would take a while but with a few screwdrivers, some connectors and electrical tape he thought that he could fix it.

The men returned to the site to tell the ladies their intentions. Mrs Saunders was relieved to hear that there may be a solution to their predicament. She told Mr Saunders how much it might cost to get them all back home. Her husband was embarrassed enough and didn't need for his wife to reveal to everybody that he had not prepared for this eventuality.

It was now almost midday so Mrs Saunders paid for some rolls and she and Phyllis proceeded to make some lunch. The children were happy to resume their games with the friends they had made and were more than willing to tell everybody what had happened. It took Ryan a good hour to fix the broken cables. Mr Saunders felt so guilty. He did not have the necessary skill to undertake such a repair. He stayed with Ryan asking him about his time in the army and passing to him the tools he needed. It was 3pm when the van was ready to be hooked up again. Already two more vans were waiting to cross the bridge to get to Camus. Norman couldn't believe his luck, so many new faces to see, he would have to be at his best. Mr Saunders got back into his car. Reg and Ryan had pulled the caravan off the verge and back onto the road but there was no option but to reverse the van all the way back to Camus. To Norman's annoyance, Ryan herded him towards the site and away from the bridge. Ryan had already opened Reg's gate so that Mr Saunders could get back in, so in consolation, Norman decided to grasp the opportunity on offer!

The Saunders decided to stay an extra night. It was too late now to start their journey home and anyway Mr Saunders felt tired after the eventful day. Reversing the caravan uphill for several hundred yards was quite daunting. Even with both Reg and Ryan shouting out instructions it was hard to keep the outfit straight. The occupants of the other vans, patiently waiting to cross the bridge, were watching intently. In the meantime, no-one was aware that Norman had reached the steading! The campers had gone down to the shore to watch the kayak races, inadvertently leaving the steading door wide open. Norman couldn't resist going inside again, leaving muddy hoof prints all over the floor. It must have seemed very different to the way he remembered it and it smelt different too. He went to the window licking it as if to explore the new panes of glass and he simply couldn't resist the wild flowers which Phyllis had placed in a vase on the table, they were just too tempting. Crash! went the vase as it smashed to the ground. Norman was oblivious, simply enjoying the taste of the freshly picked blooms. He had eaten similar ones growing in his field but as a consequence they were long gone. Water had emptied from the vase and was now running across the table.

When the campers returned, they realised their mistake and a few of the guys were brave enough to go in and attempt to shoo him out. Norman was caught unawares by their sudden entry and hurried to get back outside knocking the bench over with his enormous bulk. Although worried by the broken vase the campers could see the funny side of the whole fiasco - a real "bull in a china shop!" exclaimed one of them.

The Saunders moved back onto the first available pitch. They would be off early the next morning. The new arrivals, now both a little later on site than they had hoped, were the Daveys with their three, school-aged children and the Palmers complete with two older teenagers and a baby. The Palmers also brought along two playful border collies. Both families had been waiting across the bridge for a good hour before the Saunders' van cleared the way. There were only a few pitches left to choose from so Phyllis agreed to give them some time to settle in. She suggested that they come back to the reception when they were ready to be shown around the site.

Mr Saunders predicament was now the hot topic for everyone at Camus, thanks to his children proudly spreading the word. A few fellow caravanners came over to him, with several recounting similar stories at other locations. He was still embarrassed but heartened to hear that he was not alone. Others had even had their vans written off as a consequence. Perhaps he should think himself lucky after all. He went back to the reception to look for Reg and Ryan. He was indebted to them and wanted to pay them both for their time and trouble. Neither man would accept anything, assuring him that they would do the same for any of their guests. They were only too happy to be of assistance and so pleased that no-one had been hurt. Although Reg knew that he would have done the same for anyone, he liked to think that, in a funny way, he was already showing the same qualities that he had experienced in other true highlanders, a genuine willingness to help and pool knowledge when the need arose. At least Mr Saunders felt that it warranted an entry in the visitor book recounting his disastrous tale and the support given freely by both Reg and Ryan.

Before Phyllis could conduct her usual tour for the new guests, several apologetic campers crept into the reception to tell her about Norman's destruction in the steading. She immediately made her way there, dreading what she would find, but apart from the muddy floor and the remaining fragments of vase, the campers had done their best to tidy it up. One of her cushions had obviously ended up on the floor and was clearly showing the signs of Norman's muddy hooves but a quick wash would soon rectify that. Compared to the other events of the day, Phyllis considered that they had got off lightly. By now, Norman was over the far side of the campsite and had been spotted by Donnie who was coaxing him out with a handful of pellets.

The Daveys and the Palmers were happy to be shown around together. The younger children had run off and were being taken to all the best places by those now familiar with the site. The Palmers temporarily shut their two dogs in the van whilst the adults, teenagers and the baby all tagged along. Phyllis learned that the baby was called Macie and she belonged to the eldest daughter, Beth. Macie was only nine months old and the Palmers were now proud grandparents. Phyllis couldn't tell how old Beth was but she looked as if she were only about 18. It was obvious from their conversation that both girls were still living at home. There was no mention of Macie's dad so Phyllis made sure that she avoided the subject. They seemed impressed by the shower block and when Phyllis took them to see the steading she felt compelled to apologise for the apparent state of disrepair, courtesy of Norman, which the guests considered was highly amusing.

The Saunders left early the following morning having double-checked that their van was securely hitched. The site was busier than ever and most of the guests were off enjoying themselves. Ryan came to the reception to ask Phyllis if he could borrow her car. Of course he could but Phyllis was curious to know where he was going.

"Just going to the village to meet up with a friend" Ryan said.

Phyllis's motherly intuition immediately picked up on Ryan's use of the word 'friend' but, quashing her compelling desire to ask "who?", she decided to keep quiet, for now!

The Palmer's border collies were both young and playful and usually tethered on long leads to a stake hammered into the ground. They were eager to go for a run and Phyllis could see that Mrs Palmer was now heading off with them to the shore. A simple walk along the beach was not enough for these energetic dogs. They needed to be constantly active and kept occupied. Fortunately Mrs Palmer was a slim lady and seemed to be very fit. She was carrying a frisbee so clearly the dogs intended to play. She launched the frisbee, both dogs anxiously waiting, eyes bright and ears pricked. They set off in pursuit, obediently returning the toy and dropping it at Mrs Palmer's feet, ready for the next chase. Phyllis hoped that the dogs would not cause problems with Angus's sheep which were quietly grazing in the nearby fields. As Mrs Palmer returned to her van Angus pulled onto the site. He had met her walking back along the road and had politely asked her to keep the dogs on a lead when near any livestock. Angus also suggested places where she could take them to run free. He had had a few unfortunate experiences in the past with dogs belonging to Camus visitors but that was a while ago and he was keen to keep it that way. It was soon obvious though that the collies were well trained and, when back on the site, they were always kept on a lead.

The two teenage girls had booked a session kayaking with Donnie, leaving Macie with nanny and granddad. They thoroughly enjoyed the experience. Beth particularly welcomed the opportunity to be free again without the responsibility of Macie and the grandparents seemed more than happy to push Macie along the lane in her buggy.

The Daveys family were out and about too, visiting the lighthouse and taking Jimmy's ferry to Mull to visit Duart Castle for the day. There was so much to do from Camus when the weather was good.

Later that day a delivery arrived from Travis Perkins with materials to build the new BBQ. Ryan could hardy wait to get started and within a couple of days he was seen from the reception window admiring his fine finished project. A few minutes later he was joined by his mum carrying two piping hot cups of coffee.

"My oh my, your father will be so proud of you, you've done a great job"

"How could I have failed, it was built to Dads perfect drawings, replied Ryan with a glint in his eye"

Mum and son chatted for a while, when finally Ryan told his mum about the really lovely girl he had met at The Dobhran.

"She's called Rajakumari, Raj for short; we've decided to pop over to Mull for a couple of days. I've booked us a room at one of the hotels at Tobermory"

Ryan knew full well what was coming next, and he wasn't wrong.

"How old is she?" was Phyllis's first question.

"She's 25 and is teaching at Camran's school. Her family originally came from Pakistan but she was born near to London" Ryan revealed, pre-empting some of Phyllis's expected questions.

"When can we meet her?" asked Phyllis enthusiastically.

"She's coming to Meg's to pick me up on Wednesday so we may get time to pop in before catching Jimmy's ferry. But Mum please don't expect us to stay too long. I know what you're like!" Ryan answered cheekily.

"What do you mean by that?" Phyllis asked indignantly.

"Well you do love to rabbit for ages" Ryan replied "and we will have a ferry to catch!"

Ryan had booked a place on Jimmy's ferry as they were planning to take Raj's car. They would stay on Mull for two nights, coming back on the Friday. Phyllis wondered whether he had said more to Meg. She would find out when the friends were next on the phone.

On the Wednesday, Phyllis made sure that she looked her best and told Reg to put on his clean overalls which she had just ironed. Ryan had of course told his dad where they were going but he had not been subjected to the same barrage of questions that he had received from his mum. They pulled up in Raj's old car and Phyllis and Reg came out of the reception to greet them. Raj was stunning, tall and slender with long dark hair, neatly tied back, first in a pony tail, then pinned up behind. She had a soft voice and a beautiful smile.

Phyllis offered to make tea but the couple were anxious to go. They had just called in on their way to the ferry.

"I've heard so much about Camus from people at the school" she said "but I only started in June so I haven't had a chance to stop by. I'm teaching Camran at the moment and he's told me all about you, the film and the TV crew".

"Ryan must bring you over one evening. We've got the programme on DVD, it's really good. Do you like wildlife?" asked Reg.

"Yes" Raj replied "I'm hoping to see lots on Mull. I'd love to come back and see you both for a bit longer when we return."

Ryan took her by the hand and they made their way back to the car. They looked very happy as they went out of the gate with Raj turning her head to wave goodbye. Phyllis loved to see her son so cheerful. He deserved to be after all that he had endured. It may only have been brief but, from first sight, Phyllis had a good feeling about Raj.

"So, what do you think?" Phyllis asked Reg.

"She seems very nice and very pretty" said Reg "I hope they have a good time."

The couple caught Jimmy's ferry and landed at Tobermory where they had booked a hotel. They had agreed to take a whale-watching trip that very afternoon and then drive all the way to the other end of the island the next day, as Raj particularly wanted to visit the beautiful island of Iona.

Raj and Ryan shared a real passion for the outdoors. Raj had applied for the job at the local school even though her old Uni. friends had told her that it was very remote. When she had arrived she was mesmerised by the beauty and tranquillity and the friendliness of the village - so very different from the busy east end of London where her family still lived. She had gone to university in Edinburgh which had, by distance, broken her ties to London and she could not ever imagine going back. Ryan talked about his parents' latest plans. When they first took up the position as wardens at Camus, he had to admit that he thought they had taken on a hopeless cause but he too was amazed when he first saw the place and could now fully understand their desire to stay. Ryan and Raj got on so well and had so much in common. Ryan was obviously fit and athletic and Raj loved to walk and indeed run. She used to be in a running club at Uni. and had managed several half marathons, at various locations around the country.

The first afternoon they boarded a boat in Tobermory harbour and were taken out, along with several other tourists, to see if they could spot any dolphins, harbour porpoises or even Minke whales. The crew had a great book with laminated pictures of both mammals and sea birds to watch out for. They also told them to observe the activity of the birds as they could be a good indicator of any mammal activity. The birds would gather at any chance of feeding off the scraps left behind. Armed with binoculars, they stood on deck scanning intently all around. The boat moved further out to sea and the water became even choppier. Ryan attentively offered his support to Raj as the motion of the boat occasionally caught her off balance. There was only a brief spotting of a porpoise but plenty of sea birds. Ryan was quickly learning how to recognise the different species - cormorants, shags, razorbills, guillemots and even the differences between species of what he had previously only thought of as 'gulls'. There was the common gull, the greater and lesser black-backed gulls, the kittiwake, the herring gull and so it went on.

When they returned, Ryan and Raj were a bit disappointed that they had not seen any whales but the experience of the boat trip alone had certainly been worth it. Just before they reached the harbour, the crew spotted something in the trees high on the cliff tops and turned the boat towards the shore. A white-tailed sea eagle was soaring high over the water with its characteristic white fanned tail and distinctive huge yellow talons. Everyone pointed their binoculars in the direction indicated by the crew. Ryan spotted it first and helped Raj to guide her to the amazing creature. It was spectacular, with a wingspan of about eight feet. It was not obviously sweeping down to the water to fish but simply soaring overhead. They had considered whether to go to the nearby bird hide to see the sea eagle but had chosen the boat trip instead. What a bonus! They may not have encountered any whales but they were certainly privileged to have seen this iconic bird. The crew mentioned that a pair had been nesting above the cliffs just outside Tobermory for the last three years but all too often it was raining and the birds strangely had an aversion to getting wet but today it was bright and sunny.

That evening they enjoyed a fantastic seafood meal in their hotel. Ryan told Raj that he was staying at Megs for the time being but that he would have to think about where he would live long term and also he needed to get a job. At the moment Reg had a number of tasks lined up for him, and Donnie occasionally asked for his help too, but that would only last until the main season ended. Raj was secretly hoping that he wouldn't move away and Ryan too was feeling that there was now another reason for him to settle close to Camus.

The next day was an early start, travelling by car to the other end of Mull to catch the short ferry to Iona. They were captivated by the beautiful turquoise sea and the pristine white beaches on Iona's shore. They left the car on Mull at the Fionnphort ferry as visitors are not permitted to take vehicles on to the island without a special permit. Anyway they were happy to walk, hand in hand, along the quiet Iona lanes taking in the famous Abbey on the way. The Abbey is one of the most historic and sacred sites in Scotland. Founded by St Columba in AD563 and, to this day, is still the subject of many a pilgrimage. Neither Ryan nor Raj considered themselves to be religious but they loved to visit places with such history. Iona is also of course famous for corncrakes and the couple could clearly hear their rasping sound in the green fields surrounding the Abbey. The birds are elusive, easier to hear than to see. Ryan peered over the wall and briefly saw the small brown bird as it ran from one patch of vegetation and quickly disappeared into the next. There was no time to get a picture but simply to spot it, however brief, was a real treat.

Leaving the groups of tourists at the abbey, the couple sought their own space and made their way across the island to the Atlantic shore. There the beaches came alive with the spectacle of huge waves, rolling in from the vast ocean, finally crashing into the cliffs, sending plumes of white spray high into the air. Ryan thought that Camus was beautiful and that nothing could surpass it but he was clearly wrong. The beauty of both Mull and Iona were something else.

They sat, completely alone, on a wooden bench, gazing out to the Atlantic.

"This place has a special calming feel don't you think?" Raj said as she hugged Ryan's arm.

"I was just thinking something similar. So far removed from the places in which I have sadly spent much of my time" Ryan replied.

The pair stayed there for a good half hour almost unable to drag themselves away from such a special place but they were mindful of the last ferry back to Mull and, although neither wanted to let on, they were both looking forward to another intimate evening back at their hotel.

The next morning started with a traditional Scottish breakfast in their hotel including bacon, egg, Lorne sausage, black pudding, tomato and tattie scones complete with toast made from home-made bread. Raj was not a lover of black pudding but Ryan was only too keen to help out. In the army he had quickly learned not to let anything go to waste. After breakfast they thanked their hosts, packed their bags and made their way to catch Jimmy's ferry.

Before long they were back on board Jimmy's boat, heading back to Camus. The romantic short break away was coming to an end but, unbeknown to the happy couple, life-changing events were about to unfold. On the way back, Jimmy took Ryan to the bridge for a good long chat about his intentions for the future. Raj stayed below enjoying a nice warm coffee, keeping inside avoiding the chill of the sea breeze. Ryan revealed to Jimmy that he was quite captivated by the area, not to mention Raj of course. He was conscious though that he needed to find work which was not easily available in the area. Jimmy had a few suggestions for him. He had recently seen an advert in The Oban Times asking for a 'Senior Estate Officer' on Niall's estate and suggested that Ryan should make enquiries.

# KEEPING IT IN
# THE FAMILY

Great progress had been made while Ryan and Raj had been away. A site for the new house had been chosen, with Reg and Phyllis preferring the field between Camus and Angus's house, captivated by the wonderful views. It was only 500 yards from Camus and Angus had suggested that Reg could make a driveway just behind the current workshop. When Ewan, the surveyor, arrived one evening to mark out the boundaries the reality of their decision finally dawned on Phyllis. She had the sensation of butterflies in her stomach, not caused by anxious anticipation but rather by childish excitement bursting to be set free.

Since July, Reg had sat through many sessions with Alec, the architect, Ewan and Angus. At the start of August, Angus had submitted plans to The Highland Council and also the application to de-croft the plot. All they now had to do was to wait and, of course, consider where they might live through this winter.

The rest of August simply sped past and although the nights were beginning to draw in, Phyllis liked nothing better than to spend the evening wandering around the plot considering the best position for the house. She loved to go down to the water's edge, sit on the rocks with a cup of coffee and watch the sunset. She never tired of observing both the wagtails and the sandpipers, both of whom combed the shoreline with their characteristic bobbing, rarely still, and darting from one rock to another as if they were worried that they might miss out on something. It would not be long before the birds would leave Camus to follow the warmth they needed to see them through the winter.

Ryan had been quick to follow up Jimmy's suggestion regarding the advert in The Oban times for a 'Senior Estate Officer'. He met many of the criteria stated in the advert which asked that applicants must have practical experience of estate work, an awareness of conservation and wildlife monitoring and experience of tractor driving. It also stated that the job would require the use of chainsaws and spraying equipment and that applicants must be prepared to work outdoors in all weather conditions and possess a clean driving licence. The duties of the position included tree management, fencing, management of wildlife, attention to drainage; mechanical repairs, property maintenance, vermin control, and such other duties as may be instructed. All of these tasks would be well suited to Ryan, many of which he had done before in the army. He sent a formal application which, little did he know, would be read and considered by Niall himself. He didn't tell Reg or Phyllis though. He was still nervous about applying for work outside the Army and was secretly fearful of rejection.

When Niall received the application he couldn't believe his luck. Ryan was Reg's son and Niall greatly admired what Reg had achieved at Camus. He hadn't yet met Ryan but was aware from the local grapevine that Ryan was strong, hardworking and had the same military background as Reg, a bonus to any employer. He had also heard whispers that Ryan was dating a local teacher and therefore there might well be a chance that he would stay around for some time. He therefore wasted no time in contacting Ryan to arrange an interview. As expected, Ryan impressed and sailed through the interview process. Niall was more than happy to organise instruction on the use of a chainsaw with all the Health and Safety implications and their discussions also included Ryan's suitability to help out with the seasonal deer stalking although there was a lot of banter between Niall and Ryan about competition with his father.

Although the advert did not mention accommodation, Niall was keen to provide an incentive for him to settle so he asked Ryan where he would be living. Ryan was currently still at Meg's B&B but Niall was aware that he needed to find something more permanent.

"We have a few nice estate cottages for some of our staff" said Niall. "We could sort you out one if you are interested"

"That would be great" was Ryan's immediate response.

"So, if you're happy, all I need to ask you now is - when can you start?" said Niall as he stood up and held out his hand to seal the deal.

"I've got a few jobs to help Mum and Dad with, one of which is that I've promised to help them move their things from Worcester but apart from that I can start straight away" Ryan replied brimming with enthusiasm.

"Well let's say 1st September then" suggested Niall. "How about that?"

This proposed start date was only a few days away just after the bank holiday. Before returning to Camus to tell his parents, Ryan went straight to meet Raj. She was the most important person that he wanted to share his news with. Raj was so happy, the new term at school had started and now it seemed that Ryan's future in the area was also settled. Although they had only been dating for the last month, Ryan was already wondering whether the estate cottage might be big enough for two.

Back at Camus, Reg and Phyllis were busy preparing for the approaching bank holiday and Donnie was pleased to see Ryan as he needed some help with the kayak bookings over the weekend. Fortunately the site was expected to calm down the next week with the children back at school.

Camus would then revert to the adult quiet time as the season wound down.

Eager to share his news, Ryan suggested that they all took a tea break and he went to put the kettle on. When he had the full attention of his parents, he couldn't hold back.

"I've got an announcement" he blurted out "I've just been offered a job".

"Where?" asked Phyllis almost dreading the response.

"A Senior Estate Officer on Niall's estate" replied Ryan proudly. He then went on to tell them the details about the job and the estate property that would come with it. He left out the deer stalking though!

"You didn't tell us you'd applied" said Reg puzzled.

"I didn't know if I'd get it. I guess I was a bit nervous but I'm over the moon. I've already told Raj" he revealed, immediately realising that this might have been rather insensitive.

Phyllis was initially surprised that she was clearly not the first to know but she had already accepted Ryan and Raj as an item and was simply happy to hear that her son was now settling near Camus.

Donnie was happy for his friend, especially knowing that, come September, the kayak trips would settle down and that he would be able to manage on his own as he had before. He would miss Ryan's regular company but agreed that their regular visits to The Dobhran inn would simply have to continue. This bank holiday weekend was particularly busy for Donnie, who had another party of Uni. students booked in. The word on Facebook was spreading fast and several students were due to come camping before the new term started in mid-September.

Ryan and Raj thoughtfully paid a visit to Jimmy and Joyce, to tell them that Ryan had indeed been offered the job. Ryan wanted to thank Jimmy personally before the news filtered through the local grapevine. Both Jimmy and Joyce were proud of him and looked forward to having him around permanently. For such a sleepy place, news of Ryan's success certainly travelled quickly around Camus. Angus and Elaine heard the news from Donnie that same evening, Meg heard it on the phone from Phyllis within hours and even a few of the caravanners were officially informed by Phyllis when they collected bread the following morning.

Camus was full to the brim for the final bank holiday weekend of the year. Ryan was on call to help Donnie and, in addition to the normal weekly BBQ scheduled for Thursdays, it was agreed to lay on another for the Saturday. The students came with tents and spent many enjoyable hours in the kayaks. Children's laughter filled the air as they raced around the site. Teenagers tended to gather in the steading, stealing some space from their parents whilst charging laptops and games consoles. Several teenage crushes had blossomed within those walls, only to be cruelly shattered when the time came for the caravans to leave. No doubt the text messages would continue long after the holidays had ended. Phyllis often wondered whether any lasting romances had ever been forged at Camus.

Sometimes, though fortunately rarely, sad events had occurred at Camus, for example the death of the Norris dog. Mr and Mrs Norris arrived in an old two berth caravan that they had enjoyed for many years and it was clear when they arrived that the dog was old and fragile. He was a brown Labrador, considerably overweight and now with limited mobility. His name was Bracken and severe arthritis had resulted in stiffness in his back legs. Phyllis could see that Mr Norris had to lift him in and out of their caravan. For most of the day Bracken slept on a comfy blanket outside but in all other respects he seemed quite happy.

"How old is he?" asked Phyllis when Mrs Norris came to the reception for milk.

"He's ten now but he's been caravanning since he was a puppy and he absolutely loves it" replied Mrs Norris, or Gwen, as Phyllis had been told to call her.

"We asked our vet whether we should take him on holiday. He said 'Yes' there's no telling how much longer he has left to enjoy, but now he seems to be going downhill fast. We've changed his diet. We give him glucosamine every day and we only take him on short walks."

As the week went on it was becoming obvious that Bracken was not at all well. Every day Gwen or Trevor could be seen washing covers or towels which Bracken had been laying on during the night. The short walks had stopped and

Gwen was looking quite distraught. Finally Trevor came in to the reception.

"Do you have a phone number for the nearest vet?" he asked.

"Yes we do" replied Phyllis, not wanting to ask him why.

"Bracken's not good" he went on "he's not eaten for the last few days and now he's not drinking. We can't let this go on; Gwen is beside herself. We haven't got any children and Bracken is our baby. Perhaps we should never have come away". He asked if he could use the phone and Phyllis discretely went outside tending her baskets and giving him the privacy to make the call.

"They've told me to bring him straight down" he told Phyllis as he made his way from the reception.

Phyllis watched from her window as Trevor lifted Bracken in to the car. Gwen kept her face hidden, no doubt she had been crying. When the couple returned there was no Bracken and the pair simply retreated quietly to their van. It was two days later when Gwen came in to the reception. Phyllis dreaded asking what had happened but fortunately Gwen had pulled herself together enough to update her. The vet had advised that as Bracken had stopped eating and drinking and was also incontinent it would be kinder to put him to sleep. They were having the dog cremated in order to take the ashes back to their garden in Cheshire so they would be leaving Camus the following day, collecting Bracken's ashes on the way home.

Phyllis expressed her sorrow and asked if there was anything she could do. She thought it totally inappropriate to ask whether they had enjoyed their stay. When the subdued couple finally departed Phyllis simply wished them a safe journey home.

Ryan had started his new job and, as expected, it was as if he were made for it. Niall was impressed with the pace at which he could undertake every task and was even having to encourage him to slow down. Ryan loved outdoor physical work even when the weather was bad. Reg was receiving informal feedback from Niall, but even without that, he could tell that his son was happy.

Ryan's cottage was stunning, enjoying idyllic views all around. It was nestled in a glen on the far side of the estate where he and Raj could walk for miles from the doorstep. Running through the glen was a fast-flowing river, constantly fed by small burns squeezing water from every crevice in the surrounding hillsides. There was almost always the soft steady sound of a trickle coming from all around. After a period of rain, this sound intensified as the burns raced to deposit their increased load into the river which ran right through the glen, sometimes racing over rocks and boulders set deep in the bed below and in other places forming quiet pools resting near the bank. The water, tinged brown by the peaty soil through which it has passed on its journey from the mountains, was a favourite spot for dippers. Their pure white throat and breast made them easy to watch as they search for insect larvae and freshwater shrimps under the water.

A well maintained woodland path led from the cottage to a clearing which, Ryan had been told, was destined to be covered by a profusion of wild flowers in the spring and summer. Raj was really looking forward to smelling the delightful fragrances contained within the glen.

Being a 'Senior Estate Officer', Ryan had exclusive fishing rights to the estate's lochs and rivers, although he knew that fishing was not for him. Sitting motionless for hours, requiring undue patience, was not exactly in keeping with his character. Now that it was September, he was looking forward to welcoming the changing colours and he couldn't wait for the first signs of snow high on the tops. There was a fresh crispness in the air each morning and the evenings were drawing in fast.

Raj loved the cottage and the glen and was particularly captivated by the rowan trees, now with bright red berries hanging like jewels from every branch. Soon these berries would become a true feast for the birds. The rowan trees seemed to like nothing better than to lean over the tumbling burns and the berries added yet another vibrant colour to the start of the autumnal harvest.

The cottage itself was ideal, comprising a cosy sitting room with a wood burner and a small kitchen, just perfect for two. A spiral staircase lead to a galleried bedroom with a 5ft bed and a bathroom with shower. Quaint dormer windows protruded from the tiled roof. It was truly a picture-postcard cottage. It had previously been let as a holiday cottage so the furnishings were top class. All Ryan had needed to do was move his own personal things in. Raj was still paying for digs in the village but was spending more and more time at the cottage with Ryan. Their 'gingerbread' cottage was romantic and even though it was miles away from the nearest neighbours she felt safe, secure and warm, especially when Ryan was around.

September passed by quickly. Ryan was given quite a sizeable list of works by Niall. Firstly he was off to cut down some trees that were deemed at risk of falling, even before the inevitable winter storms arrive. Nothing much got wasted on Niall's carefully managed estate. Almost every scrap of timber felled is put to good use. Wood not destined for the mill was cut up, stored, and then used to heat the many estate buildings, including Ryan's own cottage. Niall had many a soft spot however. His empire had to run smoothly and efficiently but he had traditionally looked after some of the old folk down in the village. Ryan was told to make sure that Niall's 'old faithfulls', many of whom were retired estate workers, were kept stocked with a generous supply of logs for their fires. These were to be pre-cut to size then seasoned and delivered completely free of charge.

Ryan's next job was to fence off a plantation earmarked for new trees and shrubs. In excess of 600 posts had arrived by lorry and been transported to the area and lowered to the ground by a hydraulic grabber. They were pointed at one end, looking like giant wooden pencils. Each post had to be secured into the ground, the first stage of a deer-proof fence. Unless the deer were excluded from the area, the new shoots and saplings would not be given the opportunity to grow. In the highlands managing the deer population is an important part of any estate worker's job. Ryan had also been asked to help Niall with a new initiative - 'Wildlife Safaris'. This was in response to an increased interest in the wildlife and especially in the deer rutting season. Tourists were keen to come to shoot the deer but with cameras, not guns. For now the safaris were once a week on a Friday. Erecting the fence and driving the wildlife safaris had meant that Ryan was not asked to help Niall with any stalking. Just as well, as he would not have wanted to encroach on his father's patch. Reg was still quietly revelling in the admiration he was receiving regarding his shooting skills and Ryan was happy to leave things exactly as they were. The stalking season lasted several weeks from the beginning of September and continued until mid-October. Reg would often help out as the caravan site was now quieter and Phyllis could manage without him.

As the month went on, Reg thought that he should also start to consider where he and Phyllis might live whilst their new house was built. Meg had offered that they could stay with her but Reg, as much as he was very fond of Meg, secretly thought that he would find it too difficult to live in the same property with that incessant chatter, so independently he asked Niall whether there were any other empty properties on the estate that they might rent for say six months. In the meantime, Phyllis had been talking to Joyce and found out that Joyce's friend Pat might be happy to rent out the upstairs apartment of her croft house just along the coast from the ferry. Joyce contacted Pat to make enquiries. Pat was obviously keen because she wasted no time and quickly rang Phyllis to ask if they would like to come and have a look.

Well, as soon as they arrived at Pat's beautiful croft with its stunning views across the bay and its beautifully manicured gardens they were quite captivated. As is so typical of properties in this area, Pat usually rented it out as a holiday let. She had already taken bookings from repeat customers but it would be free from the last week in October. Camus would still be operating until that time so that would fit in nicely and it was only ten minutes drive in the car from the site.

There was a shared front door but, once inside, Reg and Phyllis would have use of the entire upstairs taking full advantage of the views from both the living room and bedroom windows. The croft furnishings were a little dated but immaculately kept and it certainly felt homely. They thought that they had been spoilt for views at Camus but they had soon come to realise that breathtaking panoramas were all around.

From the lounge window they could see across the single-track road to fields of sheep grazing in front of the shore, with the hills of Mull providing the distant backdrop. From the kitchen window at the rear there were equally peaceful, yet closer, views of the sheep whose field butted up directly to the back wall. Outside, the small road lead to a stony beach where several colourful boats were hauled up, leaning characteristically to one side. No doubt they were used for shrimps or lobsters. Indeed Angus probably knew exactly who they belonged to. They created an idyllic picture likely to be prized in many a visitor's photo album.

For Pat the opportunity to earn extra rent through the winter would be a real bonus. For Phyllis and Reg it would also be ideal; near enough to Camus to keep an eye on the build progress, close to the village and to both Meg and Joyce. Pat was a little worried when she had to tell them that she had already taken bookings for the following March.

"That's fine" said Reg "with any luck our house might be ready but if not we can get the caravan out of the workshop. We usually spend March back at Camus anyway, preparing for the new season".

They spent the evening with Pat telling her about their plans. She was a lovely lady, a similar age to them. She recounted her history of how she came to convert the upstairs floor as a self-contained holiday let, once her children left home. Business was slow to start almost ten years ago but now she received bookings from many return customers.

She had obviously heard a lot about the Camus site and how it had brought more visitors to the area. At the end of a long chat, Reg and Phyllis agreed that the croft would be ideal to see them through the winter so they agreed a price with Pat and a date for moving in, 4th November.

Camus was still open to guests through October with Annie and the children expected for the half-term week. Before then, Reg and Phyllis still had a few guests to welcome. Typically the late season visitors were mainly older couples who were usually no trouble but this year a couple arrived, Mr and Mrs Caulfield from the borders. They were well in their 70's and when they arrived it soon became obvious that they had difficulty hearing. Both were wearing hearing aids and Reg had to ask several times whether they required any help setting up. Whenever they came to the reception Phyllis made sure that she spoke slower and louder so that they could hear what she was saying.

"Do you want skimmed milk or full fat?" she asked.

"Yes I have to try hard to keep my weight down" was Mrs Caulfield curious reply.

"Where can we go to get a good meal?" asked Mr Caulfield.

"Well you'll probably be too late for the ferry boathouse now so the best place is the Dobhran" answered Phyllis.

"No I don't want to catch a ferry" replied Mr Caulfield "just get a good meal."

Both Reg and Phyllis could see the funny side but they did not envisage the problems that the Caulfields might present each evening. They clearly loved to play music in their van. They were partial to the tunes from the 50's but they turned the volume up so loud that it was a real problem for the few other guests on the site. Phyllis could hear it clearly in her own van parked some distance away!

"Strooth" exclaimed Reg "We'll have the others complaining. I don't think they realise how loud it is."

"You'll have to go and speak to them" suggested Phyllis not wanting to volunteer herself.

Reg made his way towards the Caulfield's van, thinking hard about how he could broach the subject sensitively. He tapped on their door but there was no response. He knocked again having waited for a break in the music. Mr Caulfield opened the door with a big smile.

"I wonder if you can help me out, you see I've got a bit of a problem" started Reg.

"What is it?" asked Mr Caulfield.

"I'm afraid that your music is a bit too loud" started Reg, deliberately lowering his voice to no more than a whisper.

"Sorry Reg" interrupted Mr Caulfield "I've taken out my hearing aid. We like to do that in the evening to give us a break from the whistling."

"That explains why your music is so loud then" Reg laughed. "I'm sure that you didn't realise and that you didn't mean to upset the other guests. You're lovely people and I know that you wouldn't want to do that."

Mrs Caulfield offered him a cup of tea which Reg accepted to show that there were no hard feelings. It transpired that the Caulfields had no idea of the effect their music had on others. Mrs Caulfield was so apologetic. It was obvious that they were embarrassed and so to ease the uncomfortable situation, Reg complimented them on their choice, especially the 50's which was his era. He even joked about looking forward to his own loss of hearing as it would mean that he didn't have to listen to Phyllis's constant chatter but they had to promise not to repeat his thoughts to Phyllis when they saw her next. Before Reg left they agreed to listen to their music, in future, with their hearing aids in. They went on to tell him how they bought ones with a volume control which they could adjust and asked him to stay while they played a CD, getting Reg to go outside and let them know if it was now ok.

Reg moved a short distance away from their van and when Mr Caulfield appeared at the door to gauge the reaction Reg was pleased to report that all was well. He bade them goodnight, saying that they would hear no more about it. As he walked away he chuckled at his parting statement "hear no more about it". "What a lovely old couple" he thought, pleased that a tricky situation was resolved so simply.

# STAKING A CLAIM

October came, the site was slowing down but progress was being made elsewhere. The Worcester bungalow was now sold and therefore the funds for the new build were ready and waiting. Phyllis had initially thought that she would be sad to see the Worcester bungalow go but she hardly gave it a passing thought. Inexplicably she now felt a real sense of belonging at Camus. Content with their decision to make it their permanent home, she was simply looking forward to the future.

She hoped that the rest of the season would pass quickly as she counted down the months she would have to wait for her new home. Ground works were due to start as soon as soon as they received the required permissions but Angus and Reg kept telling her that there might be a harsh winter to come. If the relevant permissions were granted it may well be possible to dig the footings in October, November or December but building the house would be difficult through January and February possibly even into March.

It was therefore not possible to plan a moving-in date with any certainty.

By now guests had reduced to a mere handful. There were no more brave campers on site but a few caravanners came to see the beautiful autumn colours. With less people around, Phyllis had more time on her hands to absorb the wonders of the landscape. Autumn was certainly a stunning season. In previous years, at this point, she had been concentrating on packing everything away. Last autumn she had been busy looking after the TV crew but finally this year was quieter. The red squirrels were busy collecting and stashing nuts, the pine martens were happy to fatten up on Meg's bird table and whenever Phyllis and Reg made their regular visits to the supermarket Phyllis insisted that they take the coast road so that she could observe the grey seals arriving, preparing to bring new pups to the western shores.

There were new delights which Phyllis had never previously appreciated. Enormous rainbows with incredible intensity and frequency simply took ones breath away. She became consumed with thoughts of how many people before her had witnessed these perpetual, natural wonders: the old, the young, the rich and the poor, these amazing shows were provided for all and recognised no hierarchy. With her new-found sense of belonging, she had been truly seduced by the spell of this most majestic area.

She sat for ages in her caravan watching the October showers, interspersed with clear blue skies, as they rolled in across the sea. One minute she could be bathed in sunshine bringing warmth through the caravan window but in the distance she watched the menacing clouds racing towards her, threatening to darken the whole site. Frequent showers temporarily obscured the hills from view whilst in that brief magical moment, between rain-induced mist and sun, prisms of colour came into view. Often only a fraction of a rainbow could be seen, leaving Phyllis to guess where it might end. Sometimes a single arch spread across the sea but quite often there were at least two, maybe three, together. Her favourite was a lingering rainbow which started at the shore line and spread over Reg's workshop into the field behind. Although she could not see from her van where it ended, she felt sure that it must be on her chosen plot. If it were, she was convinced that it was a good omen although she didn't need there to be a pot of gold to make her feel any happier.

It was not only the rainbows that captivated Phyllis. She had spent many months between April and September praying that the rain would stay away, ensuring dry, sunny weather for her guests; however, when it did rain and the rivers were in spate, it brought new drama to the mountains and glens. The landscape would not be the same without the frequent deluges resulting in lush shades of green in the fields and forests. The salmon too depended on constantly running water as did the resident otter. In the rare dry spells when private water supplies ran low, it became a real cause of concern to many of their neighbours so, as September had moved on to October, Phyllis had learned to appreciate the seemingly endless bounty from the skies. Both she and Reg now had all the necessary wet weather clothing and Phyllis would often tell her visitors that "There's no such thing as bad weather, only the wrong clothing!"

Geoffrey and Ronnie had returned in order to see the greylag geese on their way from Iceland and the red grouse that began to form pairs in the autumn. They also hoped to spot a few gannets along the coast, as they are known to migrate southwards until the end of October. The enthusiastic guests were going to move on from Camus to the Cairngorms to see the ptarmigan and hopefully snow buntings, neither of which the Camus surroundings could offer. Phyllis and Reg were always pleased to catch up with them. When the two men arrived, they shared tea and cakes in the steading, allowing Reg to update them on his latest plans for a new home. When the subject came to their son Ryan and his new job on the estate, the conversation moved on to the wildlife safari trips on a Friday. Ronnie's passion was particularly the birds but Geoffrey was keen to book the trip and get some good camera shots of the stags. A quick call to Ryan's mobile secured the last two available seats for this Friday's trip.

Ryan was a fantastic guide, taking them off-road high up into the mountains to seek great vantage points. Whenever he spotted an opportunity he stopped, turned off the land rover engine and wound down the windows. The patience required for bird watching was similarly rewarded in capturing great images of the stags. Most of the party were keen photographers but Geoffrey had an additional zoom attachment which allowed him to take particularly close-up shots. He was able to count fourteen points on the antlers of one impressive stag which was actively bellowing and watching over his harem of hinds. He offered to send Reg and Phyllis a copy of the best print when he got home. Perhaps Phyllis could find an empty wall when her new home was built.

Finally it was half-term week and time for the eagerly awaited visit from Annie and the children. Annie and William were going to stay at Meg's but Ellie had asked to stay with nanny and granddad in their caravan. Craig did not want to take any more time off as he had only been in the job for a few months and had been given two weeks off for moving house so he would stay behind this time.

Phyllis was very excited and had bought a sleeping bag for Ellie which she could set up on one of the front sofas. There was also a new drawing pad and Meg had found in her loft a wooden set of Scottish wildlife stencils which her boys used to use and she gave them to Phyllis for Ellie. The set included a highland cow and an otter; though Ellie had not yet been lucky enough to see the otter, she had heard several of Meg's tales about him. According to Annie, William, was now walking and had all the bumps and scrapes to prove it.

He was a typical boy who loved to be outdoors and seemed to have a passion for seeking out the muddiest patch in which to fall over.

Phyllis's preparations had resulted in a full itinerary for the week. On the Sunday, they would spend the day together hearing Annie's news about the new house and Ellie's account of her new school and friends. Then they would take everybody to see the new house site. On the Monday, Ellie had been invited to a sleepover with Paige. The two girls were not dissimilar in age and loved to spend time with each other. Wednesday was lined up for a visit to Uncle Ryan, his new cottage and a chance to meet Raj. Thursday was lunch at The Boathouse and Friday would see them all return home to see Craig.

When Annie's car pulled up outside their caravan, both Reg and Phyllis rushed out, arms outstretched, to greet them. Ellie squealed, with excitement as always, jumping up for nanny to catch her.

"My, what a big girl, you're getting" said Phyllis "I won't be able to catch you for much longer!"

William had changed too. Showing no fear and picking up on his sister's excitement, he headed straight for granddad. Trying to run but not yet able to control the momentum, he stumbled straight into granddad's strong arms.

"Steady on son. Trying to run before you can walk" he laughed.

Reg had taken to using the word 'son' when referring to William. It seemed the manly thing to do. He wandered off with William to take him to sit on Fergal, leaving the girls to catch up. He knew that he wouldn't get a word in edgeways anyway so it was probably better for him and William to get on with 'boys' stuff'.

"So tell me all about your new school" Phyllis asked Ellie.

"It's really nice with lots of grass to play on and a climbing frame and, guess what Nanny, there's a cow just like Norman in the next field. Can we go and see Niseag and Archie? Oh and I've made lots of friends. Would you believe that my best friend's name is Meg?" exclaimed Ellie who couldn't get all her news out quickly enough.

"I'm afraid she takes after you Mum" said Annie, laughing.

"I can't understand what you're talking about" was Phyllis's tongue in cheek reply.

Annie explained that they were now well settled at the farm. Most of the boxes were unpacked and they'd even managed to decorate the children's rooms. She had lots of pictures to show them on her laptop which she'd brought with her. She was delighted with how well Ellie had settled in at her new school and she herself had made friends, sharing coffee mornings with several local mums. After a while they went out across the site to see if they could spot the highlanders in their field.

"We didn't see Norman on the bridge Nanny. Where is he?" asked Ellie.

He probably wasn't expecting you" Phyllis replied "but don't worry he's around here somewhere".

As Norman's field came in to view, Ellie could see him grazing on the far side. Niseag, Archie and all the other calves were there too. Phyllis had taken a pocket full of pellets with her and soon they all came over, Norman first of course. Phyllis passed some pellets to Ellie who insisted on poking them through the fence one at a time and watching as the animals hoovered them up. Soon Reg joined them carrying William, already splattered in mud and making his granddad equally dirty in the process.

They returned to the caravan and William went straight to the cupboard seeking the pegs. Phyllis got out the paper, pens and stencils for Ellie. Ellie was pleased to find that there was a stencil of a highlander and sat down immediately at the table to draw a picture of Norman in his field. They all enjoyed tea and scones which Phyllis had made that morning. For the children she had sorted out some chocolate buttons which they always enjoyed. Ellie was keen to find out where she would sleep and so Phyllis showed her the new sleeping bag which, come bedtime, would be placed on the sofa. Annie went outside to phone Meg and make the necessary arrangements for the evening. They would all have tea with her mum and dad then she and William would make their way to Meg's for bath time and then bed.

It was still good light so they agreed to go and see the chosen plot for the new house. Ellie skipped ahead in her spotted pink wellies. Granddad carried William who was keen to get down and was particularly fascinated by the cow pats scattered around. Reg held his hand to stop him investigating further which he clearly seemed keen to do. The plot had been staked out by Ewan with red and white striped tape, which was blowing in the cool sea breeze. Reg pointed out where each room would be and promised to show Annie a copy of the plans. Phyllis took Ellie down to the shore, pointing out the fine views.

"Will William and me be able to come and stay?" asked Ellie.

"Yes of course. You will be Nanny's very special guests" replied Phyllis.

"In my house my room is pink and William's is blue" Ellie continued.

"What colour will you ask Granddad to paint your rooms in this house?" enquired Phyllis.

Ellie looked around and was immediately struck by the sun lighting up the far off fields. "Gold for me I think Nanny and William loves his red bus so he'd probably like red".

They all enjoyed a real family evening, sharing hot buttered crumpets with cream cheese followed by Black Forest trifle, one of Nanny's specialities. Ellie happily kissed her mum and little brother goodnight as Annie headed for Meg's, saying that she would be back at 11.00 in the morning to take Ellie to Elaine's.

The nights were drawing in quickly and it was dark by 6.30. Phyllis allowed Ellie to stay up until 8.00 on the proviso that she then went straight to sleep. Ellie was surprised when Phyllis told her to put on her hat and coat but she was simply too excited to sleep anyway so she did as Phyllis asked and followed her Nan outside.

Phyllis's ever increasing appreciation of the Camus surroundings had recently encouraged her to enjoy her evening cocoa outside the van. In the complete darkness, she would simply listen to the sound of the sea as it rolled over each stone along the shore. The haunting sound of the owls was comforting and she would often spend ages trying to detect from which tree each sound might be coming. Most of all she was overcome by the stars. There was no light pollution here and on a clear night the sky became simply magical and she just had to share all this with Ellie. The two of them stood outside, hand in hand.

"Just look up Ellie and tell me what you see" whispered Phyllis.

"It's beautiful" gasped Ellie "It looks like fairy dust Nanny."

"Have you ever seen such a beautiful sky?" asked Phyllis "how many stars can you count?"

Ellie didn't reply at first but Phyllis could see that she was quietly trying to count as if she was frightened that too much noise might frighten the stars away.

"There's too many to count" replied Ellie "How many are there Nanny?"

"I don't know sweetie. More than either you or I can possibly count. Do you know why we can see so many stars here?"

"No" whispered Ellie still staring at the sky with real interest.

"Because there are no other lights to take away their magic" was her Nan's response.

They stayed outside for quite a while before coming in. Ellie quickly changed into her pyjamas and slipped into her lovely new sleeping bag and Phyllis snuggled her in for a bedtime story whilst Reg retreated to the bedroom for a quiet read. It didn't take long before Ellie's eyes closed, her breathing calmed and her exciting day was over. When Phyllis went to join Reg, she immediately sensed that nothing more needed to be said. They were clearly both content with what would be just the first of many family visits.

Ellie slept well but was up early the next morning. Fortunately both Reg and Phyllis were early risers. Ellie asked if there were any other children on the site but sadly there were none. The only visitors they still had were the occasional motor homers taking a one or two night stop.

There are many companies in Scotland who rent out motor homes to people who choose to tour around. The ability to wild camp is a real attraction to those seeking a remote, closer to nature holiday. It was not unusual for such vans to stop for a single night simply to use the facilities, to fill up with water and empty their waste but Reg didn't mind as these motor homes were frequent visitors throughout the whole season.

Some people choose motor homes as an alternative to caravans, maybe because they find towing somewhat daunting. Drivers have to be at least aged 25 plus to hire a motor home but don't need to have passed the additional test now required for newer drivers to tow a caravan. For whatever reason, hiring motor homes has become big business in Scotland. The consequence of this however, is that the drivers are often not used to either the size of the vehicle nor with the width of the roads. Camus was on a single-track road with passing places and, of course, the narrow humped back bridge. There were many occasions where two such vehicles met up along the lanes and Reg had heard humorous stories of the steps they had taken to pass each other. Several times such visitors had asked to use the telephone to report damage to the hire company caused by branches protruding from hedges or a misjudgement of width. At this late point in the season, most motor homes were hired by older couples and Phyllis loved to ask them about where they had already been and where they were now off to. This process usually took a good half hour while they were booking in. This morning there were only two motor homes on site and they would be leaving later that day.

Next morning Annie arrived with William for a quick cup of tea with mum and dad then Annie, Phyllis and Ellie took off for Elaine's. They had intended to take William with them, but the young laddie was fidgeting and holding his arms up to his granddad.

"I think he wants another go on your tractor Dad" Annie told him.

"You'd better leave him with me then" replied Reg.

So Reg was left in sole charge of William but he knew exactly what to do. With a grin from ear to ear, Reg lead William off in the direction of his beloved tractor. This time he started Fergal up which seemed to frighten William and made him cry. Reg quickly switched off the engine.

"Here, what's all that silly noise?" he asked his grandson. "Granddad's turned it off now. Let's go outside and see Norman instead."

Norman was, by now, almost as used to Reg as he was to Angus and always came right up to the fence to see if he had any pellets which Reg had often placed in his pocket. Whilst Norman searched for the treats, William was able to get his tiny hands through the fence and grab Norman's long coat. He seemed fascinated by the golden strands but had a tendency to tug rather than stroke. Reg therefore tried to distract him by getting him to poke some pellets through the fence but William seemed more intent on tasting them himself. Clearly that was not a good idea either. Finally Reg took him down the slipway to the shore where William could splash his feet in the water, immediately soaking both himself and his granddad. Reg didn't mind. He knew that he could take William straight back to the caravan and wrap him up in nice dry towels. It was just so lovely to see a little boy doing what little boys do. It reminded Reg of the games he used to play with Ryan when he was about William's age. That now seemed such a long time ago but it gave Reg another idea!

When Phyllis and Annie returned they found Granddad and William in the van with William wrapped up in one of Granddad's oversized shirts tied up neatly with string. They simply had to laugh which made William giggle. It was clear to Annie that this was only the start of a special Granddad-grandson relationship.

Annie was looking forward to meeting Raj. Phyllis was happy to fill her in with all the information including how beautiful Raj is, how lovely to speak to and how well suited she is to Ryan. She was already speaking as if Raj was a permanent feature even though the pair had only been together for three months. Phyllis had noted the change in Ryan; he was calmer and more settled. Reg soon realised that this mother and daughter chat was not what he wanted to sit around and listen to so he left William playing with the pegs while Annie sorted him out his spare clothes, leaving Reg to slip out, empty the bins and retreat to his workshop.

Ellie had a lovely time with Paige but when Annie turned up in the afternoon to collect her; Ellie was equally excited about seeing her uncle and his new girlfriend. Respecting the fact that Ryan's cottage was small, Phyllis decided that she and Reg would stay behind.

Ryan had worked longer hours on Monday and Tuesday so that he could be home earlier on Wednesday and, because it was half term, Raj was there also. Annie couldn't get over what a beautiful cottage it was.

"My God you've landed on your feet here haven't you" she said to her brother as she looked around.

"We absolutely love it" interrupted Raj. "There are some beautiful walks all around. Do you like walking?"

"Yes we do" replied Annie referring to herself, Craig and Ellie. "We carry William in a special toddler back pack but he's getting a bit heavy for me now."

Before it got dark they went outside to see the glen, the burn and the rowan trees and take in the beauty of Ryan's new playground. Raj had prepared a roast chicken, roast potatoes and vegetables. Annie told them that she was going to start her own vegetable garden and Ellie joined in saying that she would grow her own carrots. Again it was a lovely family evening, something that Annie had missed sharing with her brother whilst he was in the army. Life for everyone was changing and they all agreed that it felt good.

# HOMELESS?

It was soon time to return to Stirling but this time there were no more sad goodbyes, not knowing when the next visit would come. Annie had invited Reg, Phyllis, Ryan and Raj for Christmas and had arranged to go Christmas shopping with Phyllis before Ellie broke up from school. Christmas was now only about eight weeks away and Reg and Phyllis had to prepare to move in to Pat's on 4th November.

Phyllis continued her new-found passion for stargazing. One particular night she had forgotten and left the light on in the steading, as she had been moving some objects in from the caravan. As she was walking outside, looking up to the sky, she saw the distinctive feathers of the barn owl sweeping across the camping field and disappear into the steading eaves, the white plumage delicately reflecting the light from the windows. She was so excited that she went straight to fetch Reg and together they stood outside, hoping to watch another flight but there was no more sign of the owl and it had not been possible for Phyllis to see whether it was now in the steading or back out hunting.

She couldn't tell whether it was the same owl captured so beautifully in Geoffrey's photo but for now she preferred to think that it was.

"I can't believe that it's come back at last" she said to Reg, gripping his hand "It seems like everybody is coming home."

They dutifully kept Camus open until the end of the month but there had been no more guests for the last few days. Phyllis gave the caravan a last thorough clean before it was to go into Reg's workshop for the winter but this time he would need to site it well over to one side and towards the back, leaving space for the building materials that he was hoping to receive for the new house. He would do the usual preparations for winter, draining out all the caravan water pipes and removing the gas bottles. He was fully expecting that it would be home again in only four months time.

There were only a few days to go before they moved to Pat's, when Reg was out at dawn one morning and he also saw the owl hovering purposefully over Angus's field before diving swiftly to the ground to catch its prey. There was more evidence outside the steading where he found a few small, sausage-shaped pellets, containing the undigested parts of the owl's food. As pellets do not pass through the intestine of the bird, they are quite different from droppings. They do not smell and are not unpleasant to pick up. Reg carefully crumbled some in his hand, revealing what he thought were the bones of birds and small mammals, enclosed by softer material like fur and feathers. He reported his findings to Phyllis who was more than happy to believe him without the need to bring the evidence into her freshly cleaned caravan.

By the 4$^{th}$ November Reg had packed a few boxes containing their personal possessions and took them to Pat's. As a holiday let, the apartment had furniture and kitchen implements for their use but Phyllis had taken her own towels and bed linen. The apartment had a washing machine and while Reg kept an eye on Camus, Phyllis would look after their domestic chores. Pat's apartment was only 10 minutes in the car from the site so although Reg locked away his tools in the workshop and put the padlock on the gate, he left feeling more relaxed in the knowledge that he could return whenever he wanted - if necessary, every day.

For the 5$^{th}$ November the locals had arranged their annual bonfire on the beach. When Reg and Phyllis had visited Pat a few weeks before to agree the let, they had walked along the road and noticed the pile of branches and driftwood being purposefully built up. They considered that it was probably material collected by children and thought no more of it but now it was clear that it was an annual, local tradition. Pat told them that families turn out from all around. Some of the men prepared a BBQ, with everyone bringing along their own drink. A £5 per family contribution was usually made for fireworks and it would be a great opportunity for Reg and Phyllis to meet everybody, although they already knew most of them, especially the children at the local primary school who came to Camus earlier in the year when the TV film was screened. Still they looked forward to it. Reg asked who he should speak to to see if he could help with the bonfire. It turned out that Alasdair was the main man in the village. He usually allocated the various duties and Pat was sure that he would not decline Reg's offer of help.

The next morning Reg joined in with Alasdair to help build the casually collected wood into a secure pile which stood impressively over six feet high. He also went to the houses of people who had debris that they wanted to burn and brought it back to the beach. Reg was uncharacteristically happy to take orders. It would not seem appropriate to take control as was his penchant. Being safety conscious, he collected several buckets in which the children could deposit used sparklers, and filled each with water.

In the meantime, Phyllis and Joyce made more than 100 lemon flavoured Scotch pancakes. Phyllis was enjoying the opportunity to take part in festivities which, in previous years, they had missed.

As the evening arrived, a host of excited children gathered on the beach. When the bonfire was lit and the fireworks started, the reflections across the bay seemed to dance enthusiastically. The BBQ was enjoyed by all, with Reg doing his share of cooking. During the evening, both Reg and Phyllis got the opportunity to talk to many of the locals. The number of offers of help which Reg received relating to the building of his new home was amazing. Somehow Reg immediately realised that the offers were sincere and, although they had not yet chosen a builder, he ended the evening with offers of local help from almost every trade he was likely to need. Phyllis spent the whole evening in conversation with anyone prepared to listen, including most of the children. When the evening ended and the children were off to their beds, she helped to collect up the paper plates and cups and took all the dishes back to her apartment to share the washing up with Pat. The bonfire night had clearly been a great success.

Phyllis soon enjoyed regular coffees with Pat and went to share updates with Meg at least twice a week. Reg, on the other hand, soon felt the need to get out and get busy. He was not happy unless he had a project in which to immerse himself. He had a few jobs to tend to at Camus. The first was to lay some new hard-standings, the second was to overhaul the hook ups, and the third was to draw up plans for a greenhouse for Phyllis which he had decided to erect at the side of his workshop. He wanted to keep it a secret for her as a Christmas present so he erected hoardings all around. Phyllis was sure to make visits to Camus when the house construction started so his surprise needed to be kept out of view. With Ellie and William in mind he had also had an idea to build a play area, not only for his grandchildren but also for the benefit of next year's visitors.

The natural world continued with its well-rehearsed foxtrot of activities but for Reg and Phyllis their lives were held in an almost trance like state. For sure Reg was kept busy with his list of works at the Camus site and Phyllis with next year's bookings and endless chats with her new found village neighbours, but secretly their thoughts and hopes were consumed, not knowing whether their applications for the new house were to be granted or refused. Finally on the 11Th of November at 9.30am the door bell rang; it was Drew the Postman. He handed over two large envelopes, unable to conceal his enormous smile; he calmly whispered "the waiting is over". He tapped his hat with a gestured salute then silently and politely vanished from their view. Phyllis nervously opened the first envelope.

"Reg, it's from the Crofting Commission. Permission to de-croft has been granted" Phyllis revealed excitedly.

Unable to resist, Reg was by now flicking through the pages of the second letter.

"And this one's from the Highland Council. Guess what? They've accepted the plans".

"So when can we start?" was Phyllis's obvious question.

"Straight away I think. Can you put the kettle on dear so we can check this all out properly" suggested Reg.

"If it were later in the day I'd be more inclined to open that bottle of champagne left over from our anniversary but it's too early in the morning" said Phyllis, giggling with excitement.

They went through all the papers confirming that the necessary approvals had been granted but Reg suggested that they ring Angus and ask when it would be convenient to drop by and get him to check as he had been through it all before. Phyllis rang Elaine, having agreed with Reg that they wouldn't reveal anything over the phone. Elaine was pleased to hear that they were well settled at Pat's. She would be in all day apart from the afternoon school run and Angus was out feeding the cattle but would be back before lunchtime. Elaine therefore suggested that they should come over about midday and share some 'pieces' (sandwiches) with them.

When they arrived at Elaine's, Angus checked all the paperwork and confirmed that, yes; they were now able to start building. Now that the necessary permissions had been received, Reg would need to meet with Hamish and shake hands on the previously suggested purchase price. Reg told Angus about the local tradesmen who had offered to help when he was talking to them at the BBQ. Angus knew that work was hard to come by for the locals, all of whom he knew and could vouch for. Reg agreed that he would project manage certain elements of the build himself and between the two friends they felt that they could do a lot of the build themselves, hiring in diggers and certain other equipment. Angus still had all the records of his own build which would be extremely useful.

Reg immediately started to draft a detailed project plan, something he was very good at. Spending many hours on the computer, he listed every conceivable detail of the project. After consulting with Angus they decided to accept a quote from Tam McLean for the ground works because Tam was able to start before the month ended. This might give them a real chance of laying the foundations before Christmas. Tam's quote included the hire of a digger but with Reg and Angus agreeing to act as labourers, Tam would be able to keep the cost down. On 26th November the work officially started. Phyllis had been told to keep away and allow the boys unfettered progress.

Along with all his time spent planning the project Reg, was still able to afford some time erecting the structure of Phyllis's greenhouse. He had been advised that such a delicate building would need secure fixing as it would be subjected to the fierce Atlantic winds which had a reputation for lifting many sheds and greenhouses and bringing them crashing to the ground some distance away. Reg had observed that many locals had erected strong wooden timbers across the roof, bolted in to a concrete base. He thought that he would do the same. On one occasion, when Phyllis herself went to check up on Camus, she saw the hoarding erected along the side of the workshop. She asked Reg what it was for but he quickly explained that it was for storing materials he would need for the build. Phyllis readily accepted this and so no more was said.

Phyllis found it hard to be patient and wanted to visit the site regularly to check progress. The weather was still quite mild for this time of year but inevitably there were days when there was no news to report. It was great when Annie suggested that Phyllis go to Stirling so that they could do some Christmas shopping. Phyllis looked forward to choosing presents for the children. Her Christmas list was quite extensive now - Ryan, Raj, Reg, Annie, Craig, Ellie, William, Angus, Elaine, Donnie, Paige and Camran, Meg, Joyce, Jimmy and now also Pat. She still had a few friends in Worcester but had agreed with them all to send cards only this year. After all, what would they send to Reg or Phyllis as they were now about to have everything they ever needed?

Phyllis drove to Annie's and planned to stay for three days. Although Reg was also invited, he made his excuses. Neither he nor Phyllis had been to Annie's new home yet and Reg was really looking forward to seeing it but he needed to be at Camus helping Tam with the build and anyway shopping was not something he enjoyed.

Annie's house was a fine traditional detached farmhouse enjoying an idyllic setting. Although extremely peaceful, the property was convenient for all village amenities including local shops and a good primary school. The railway station was nearby and it was only 20 minutes drive to Craig's work.

Surrounding the property were extensive, mature gardens offering ample opportunity for the children to play. The ground floor comprised a reception hall, a lounge with dining area, a downstairs cloakroom and a stunning kitchen-diner with integrated appliances. The original farmhouse was built from lovely old stone with a recently added conservatory. Upstairs were four bedrooms, one with en suite shower room and a family bathroom. All rooms were impeccably presented with tasteful décor but Ellie couldn't wait to show her Nan her recently decorated pink room. Phyllis was so pleased to see them all happily settled and it made her even more impatient for her own new home although it would be significantly smaller than Annie's.

As planned, Phyllis, Annie and William went Christmas shopping in Stirling. It had been ages since Phyllis had browsed such wonderful shops. There was the inevitable mall, 'The Thistles', containing all the usual chain-stores and Phyllis was overcome with choice. They also made their way to 'The Old Town' near to the castle where, at last, William was set free from his buggy to totter about and chase the pigeons. Phyllis knew that Reg would particularly like the old town with all its history. Perhaps she would return with Reg at a later date but for now she and Annie were clearly on a mission to 'shop til they dropped'.

They finally gave up when William showed the same irritation with Christmas shopping as Phyllis had witnessed with his granddad. They made their way back to the car with William's buggy weighed down with bags and parcels and Phyllis almost dead on her feet. Ellie had gone to a friend's for tea and Annie prepared dinner for the adults.

The following day, Phyllis went with Annie on the school run and watched Ellie happily run into the playground.

"Bye sweetheart" she called out as Ellie turned to wave "See you at Christmas".

As expected, by late December the foundations were laid and, apart from agreeing which tasks Reg and Angus could undertake themselves, there was unlikely to be any further progress until March or at least until the weather allowed. There were still a few days to go before they were expected in Stirling. Reg was busy fitting the last panes of glass in the greenhouse. Finally he took some photos which he would give to Phyllis on Christmas day. As always, Reg was quite pleased with his work. He just hoped that Phyllis would love it and, even better, he hadn't had to browse around any shops to find her a present.

Phyllis made a final pre-Christmas visit to Meg, Joyce and Elaine, leaving presents that were to be placed under their trees. Reg and Phyllis set off from Camus on 23rd December and would be joined by Ryan and Raj at Annie's on 24th. Reg was also impressed with Annie's new house, now bedecked with Christmas decorations and a beautiful tree. William was obviously pleased to see his granddad and followed him around wherever he went. The grandchildren had so many toys to play with that Reg wondered where on earth they would find room for a whole new set on Christmas Day. He didn't have to wait long as Ellie woke everyone up at 5.30 on Christmas morning. Reg was an early riser but it had been many years since he was forced to be bright and cheerful at such an unearthly hour.

Ellie was eager to wake Uncle Ryan and Raj but Annie managed to hold her back until 6am before agreeing to take them in a cup of tea. Ryan was always a great laugh and Raj was very used to children so hopefully they would not mind.

"It's not Christmas Day yet" teased Ryan, trying to bury himself under the covers.

"Yes it is Uncle Ryan. Get up, Santa's been" screeched Ellie.

William was standing up by the bed tugging on the duvet and squealing just like his sister although he didn't really understand why.

By 7.30 everybody was dressed and gathered around the tree in anticipation.

"I think that you children should have your Santa presents now. Then after breakfast we'll see what else is under the tree" suggested Annie.

The Santa presents went down a treat although William was still fascinated equally by the tattered paper and empty boxes which were, by now, scattered all around. The adults elected to take cereal rather than take Annie away from the children to prepare a cooked breakfast. As Annie had left the turkey cooking overnight, the house was filled with the tempting aroma of Christmas and they all knew that, by the end of the day, they would have eaten more than they should.

The exchange of gifts between the family seemed to go on for ever, only interrupted by the passing round of drinks, chocolates and nibbles. The children loved their gifts and William possessively clutched the bright red digger which Nanny had chosen. Raj looked lovely with the pashmina Annie had bought her and when it came to Reg's turn to give his gift to Phyllis, he simply passed her an envelope.

"What's this" she said, as she eagerly ripped it open. Several photos fell to the floor all of which Reg had cut in two, requiring her to put the pieces together. When she first saw the greenhouse she was not immediately aware of the significance. Neither did she recognise the familiar green background of Reg's workshop but when Reg leaned over and explained what he had been up to, she welled up in tears.

"Oh Reg thank you" she said kissing him on the cheek "How on earth did you find time to do that?"

Reg simply shrugged and smiled. He just loved to see her so happy.

Phyllis reached under the tree to get her present for Reg. It was a medium sized box, giving nothing away.

"I hope that you enjoy this" she said as she passed her gift to Reg.

Reg opened it carefully, revealing a new camera clearly far better than the pocket-sized digital that he already had.

"Geoffrey told me what to get so I hope it's good" she said.

"Thank you dear" he replied "I'll look at it later when I've got time to read all about it." He put the camera back in its box and then safely behind the sofa so that it would not get damaged.

They enjoyed their Christmas dinner with all the trimmings. Phyllis and Raj helped Annie to get everything ready in the kitchen. Raj explained that she and Ryan would be going to see her family on 28th and then Ryan had surprised her by booking a two night New Year stay at a posh hotel in Perth. She had always wanted to experience Hogmanay in Scotland, knowing how well the Scots celebrate the New Year. After dinner William had his usual sleep and the men agreed to clear away the plates leaving Annie, Phyllis and Raj to play Ellie's new board game. Fortunately the rules were quite simple and Raj had played it with her school children before. Ellie actually won, probably aided by the fact that the older women were too busy talking to concentrate but in any case they all enjoyed it. The afternoon and evening continued with charades and a spot of Wii games. For charades they split into two teams, girls v boys, even though William's contribution was somewhat limited. Of course, when the girls won, poor William obviously got the blame. They had all laughed so much that Phyllis's sides hurt. Eventually it was time for Ellie to go to bed and she was allowed to choose who should read her a story. After much consideration she chose Uncle Ryan, who then chased her upstairs pretending to be a monster. Ellie squealed partly in fear and partly with excitement.

"Trust him" sighed Annie "I feel sorry for any kids he's going to have."

Raj simply sat back in her chair and smiled.

# LIVING THE DREAM

Phyllis and Reg returned to Pat's on 28th December. Just as well, as the first dusting of snow fell on 31$^{st}$. Reg had, by now, spent many hours reading the instructions which came with his new camera and took the opportunity to go to Camus and capture the white powder now covering the footings of their new home. The camera would enable him to take better, close up pictures of the wildlife, although he knew that he had a lot to learn to be as good as Geoffrey. When they got Pat on the subject of photography, it was obvious that she was no novice herself. She had a large collection of impressive photos that she had taken. Mind you, Reg had already learnt that it was not difficult to capture picture postcard scenes all over Scotland. Many of their visitors were keen photographers and every year a few guests had sent them memorable photos to add to the Camus collection.

"Do you know what tickles me?" Reg asked Pat.

"No" she said.

"You know when tourists take pictures looking up to the mountain summits, like Ben Nevis for example. Then they climb up and take pictures looking back down. Don't you think that's kinda' funny?" laughed Reg.

"Yes you're right" said Pat "I've never thought of it that way".

There was the usual New Year céilidh in the village hall. A céilidh is always a popular event in Scotland. Originally it was a form of entertainment where stories, poems and ballads were recited and songs were sung. Nowadays it mainly involves dancing. The formality of the dances varies. Some céilidhs mix modern pop music with a Scottish country dancing band and dress codes range from some being compulsory highland dress to others less formal. Céilidh music is played by an assortment of instruments: fiddle, flute, tin whistle, accordion, drums, guitar and of course bagpipes. The music is cheerful and lively, and the basic steps can be learned easily; fortunately a short instructional session is often provided for new dancers before the start of the dance itself.

Dancing at céilidhs is typically in the form of set dances or couple dances. Each couple exchanges both position and partners, while all the time keeping in step with the beat of the music. Some of the dances are named after famous regiments, historical battles and events, others after items of daily rural life for example the "Gay Gordons", "Strip the Willow" and "Dashing White Sergeant.

All the locals attended and Phyllis was encouraged by Pat to bring Angus, Elaine and family and also Ryan and Raj. Phyllis knew that Ryan and Raj had their own plans and sadly this year Hamish did not feel up to coming. He had always played the accordion but his arthritis was getting worse so Elaine had suggested that they would all stay at home; however, Phyllis was keen to join in fully at the céilidh and had sneakily practised a few of the dances in Pat's kitchen. She thought that it was about time she got a bit more proficient. The evening was great fun and Reg was quite surprised how quickly Phyllis picked up the steps! Reg did not sport a kilt although most of the locals did. He did however get out his best suit which he had little excuse to wear in recent times.

Phyllis had clearly benefitted from Pat's instruction and Reg too coped with most of the dances. Occasionally they turned the wrong way but were quickly helped by the other couples. When the dances became particularly lively there were kilts twirling in every direction! "Thank goodness that they were made of sufficiently heavy material" thought Phyllis.

The dancing went on into 'the wee small hours' interrupted only by the welcoming of the New Year. As the chiming of Big Ben sounded over the radio, Reg shared a meaningful kiss with Phyllis, whispering to her that this was sure to be a good one. Both Reg and Phyllis thoroughly enjoyed the evening, the company of the locals and the arrival of, what should be, a surely memorable year.

When Ryan and Raj returned they had enjoyed a more luxurious affair at a posh hotel. Ryan had felt uncomfortable in his suit as most of the others were wearing kilts while Raj had worn a beautiful evening dress and looked simply stunning. She had brought back the menu for the Hogmanay dinner to show Phyllis.

*Haggis, neeps and tatties, whisky cream sauce*
*Goats cheese roast pepper and tomato tart*
*Melon bathed in a raspberry coulis*
*Traditional Scotch broth*

✳

*Champagne and strawberry sorbet*

✳

*Slow roasted lamb, Stornaway black pudding*
*Roast Ribeye of Prime Scotch Beef with Roast Root Vegetables with a Mushroom & Red wine sauce. Isle of Mull Cheddar, Spinach & Walnut Bannock served on a Scottish Elderflower Wine, Cream and Herb sauce with a Parsnip & Pear Puree.*
*Lemon sole, sautéed garlic spinach, lemon and tomato butter sauce*
*Pumpkin ravioli, wild mushrooms, butternut squash, pesto sauce*
*Seasonal vegetables and potatoes*

*Homemade Clootie dumpling, vanilla custard*
*Traditional homemade cranachan, brandy snap praline*
*Selection of fine cheeses, oatcakes, grapes, homemade fresh*
*fruit chutney*

✳

*Coffee and petit fours*

They had been given a huge en-suite room and had enjoyed a full Scottish breakfast the following morning. The céilidh went on from 10pm to 2am. Their stay was finished off in true style. Whilst sharing breakfast in the hotel conservatory which looked out to the garden dusted with a thin layer of freshly fallen snow, they spotted three roe deer nervously grazing on the lawn. How iconic! Raj was truly captivated and felt that it beat any New Year in England that she had previously experienced.

As the ladies exchanged their New Year stories, both Raj and Phyllis thought that they might go to the regular Scottish dancing classes held by Pat in the church hall but they didn't start until May so whether they would stick to their intention would have to be seen.

January and February seemed to go on for ever. As expected there were times when little progress was made with the build so Reg took the opportunity to spend time researching the limpet shells he had found in the steading. He found lots of information on the internet reading that, during the mid-19th century, most crofters in the Highlands of Scotland were very dependent on potatoes as a source of food. The potato was perhaps the only crop that would provide enough food from the land but in 1846, potato crops were blighted, crops failed and the following winter was especially cold and snowy. Some crofters therefore resorted to eating foods which were not part of their normal diet. Shell fish generally, and more specifically limpets, were clearly a food that could be relied upon in times of hardship. The potato famine came not long after the collapse of the kelp industry. Both of these disasters saw the start of the Highland Clearances which Meg had spoken about so passionately when they first arrived. The rich landowners had realised that the revenue from introducing sheep returned far more than the rents received by the impoverished crofters so they started to ruthlessly clear the people from the land. During the ten years following 1847, throughout the Highlands, over 16,000 crofters were shipped overseas to Canada and Australia. By 1857, potato crops were again growing without serious blight.

Reg had also found out that an alternative explanation was that the limpet shells may have been left as a by-product of a more routine task. Their use as fishing bait is frequently mentioned in articles about Scotland. Reg preferred to think that this was the most likely explanation after all; Camus was a sincere place, holding back no secrets. Revelations of historical findings fuelled the imagination and were probably best left in the mind of the discoverer. Phyllis and Reg had, in previous seasons, the opportunity to meet several Americans and Canadians visiting in hired motor homes. Often they were searching out their ancestry and appeared to know more of the history of the Clearances than their British visitors.

There were of course some bright but bitterly cold days in these early months, which gave Reg the chance to order and spread more Type 1 gravel for his hard standings. He also checked and repaired a few electrical hook-up points which had been cracked or damaged during the last season.

Winter appeared to be the one season that Reg and Phyllis were yet to fully experience. The west coast was known to be spared the worst of the snow, compared to higher and more in-land regions, but nature has its own way of meting out its wrath. High winds in these parts were common during winter months, often attaining speeds in excess of 100 MPH. Reg had made mental notes of these conditions but he was a strong man, resourceful and very determined, therefore no traces of discontent were afforded; his thoughts were confined to an awareness of what may lie ahead, how best to react and, more importantly, how best to prepare.

On days when there were strong winds, he retreated to his workshop to make various stages of his play equipment. He built the frame for a pair of swings, one with a conventional seat and the other with a baby chair. He particularly enjoyed making a strong wooden tractor. He carved each separate piece from hardwood with the image of Fergal in mind. The tractor would later have to be set in concrete to give stability for William, and hopefully many other children, to clamber over. He also made a playhouse with seats and a table to go inside. He had an idea about using plywood for the roof and covering it each year with heather he would collect around Camus. This would create the image of the steading as Hamish had said it used to be. All these jobs certainly kept him busy although he was itching to get back to his building project.

Before Christmas, Reg had seen Hamish, agreed a price and completed the legal paperwork to officially buy both the plot of land for the house and also the Camus site. The inheritance from Phyllis's father Henry and the proceeds of selling their bungalow still left them with a healthy budget to pay for the building work and hopefully to provide for them in the years to come.

As March approached, Phyllis would look out each morning and ask whether Reg thought that the works could start. Reg did indeed make daily visits to the site. Sunrise was now at about 7am and already the days were becoming noticeably longer with sunset not until about 6pm. At first the ground was still hard and any resting water froze overnight, too cold therefore to start the brickwork.

When March finally came, it was time for Phyllis and Reg to leave Pat's and move back to their caravan so that Pat could prepare for her first holiday guests. Reg removed the unfinished play equipment in order to get the caravan out. Although the caravan had been fully cleaned before it went into storage, there were always things to sort out. Phyllis re-stocked the cupboards, filled the wardrobe and happily resumed residence, hoping that it would only be for a few more months.

Winter was slowly losing her grip, dormant life now stirring and if you looked hard, you could begin to see the first shoots of spring bulbs around the Camus site. There were crocuses, fritillaries and snowdrops all starting to cautiously pop up their heads. Yellow primroses were emerging from beneath shrubs and from under the overhanging trees near the burn. Phyllis relied upon these early enthusiasts to welcome the new season, reminding her that now was the time to start the preparations for her own displays. She was looking forward to using her new greenhouse and in particular to removing her begonia tubers from their over wintering boxes into separate pots so that they could begin to reveal the signs of new growth.

Reg too allowed himself the odd moment to gaze lovingly at Camus. On one such occasion, standing by the steading, a vision of his impending new home flashed through his mind, a strong feeling of belonging produced a free smile, aimed at no-one, for he was, after all, completely alone; his smile reflected his own inner feelings, a man utterly at ease with himself and his surroundings.

Part of Reg's planned itinerary for this season was to induct Phyllis on all the regular tasks of emptying the bins, adding chemicals to the waste water, cleaning the drains and maintaining the hot water system. He knew that he would immerse himself in the build once the work started and it was therefore important that Phyllis took on more of the routine tasks at Camus. Of course she still had the reception to run but for a while she would have to manage both. At first he took her around with him. He would watch to make sure that she was completing each scheduled task as he expected.

For the first time in their marriage it lead to a few cross words. Phyllis had her own way of doing things but if she did not stick rigidly to Reg's instructions, she could sense that he was irritated. Phyllis therefore resorted to her usual routine whereby she would follow his every word to the letter whilst he was around but then revert to 'the Phyllis' version when she was left on her own. Sometimes she lacked Reg's strength when it came to changing the gas bottles or freeing the taps but Donnie was always near at hand and, unbeknown to Reg, he had told Phyllis to ask him if anything became too much for her.

Spring was arriving unseasonally early and by the second week of March Angus and Reg prepared to start the build. Phyllis had taken bookings for the first few caravans of the year and this year Easter was falling early with school holidays starting on 5th April. It was therefore likely to be a hectic start but Phyllis knew that she would manage. Indeed she was determined to manage, leaving Reg to build the walls, fit the roof and the windows and get the new home ready as soon as possible.

Every day Reg was up before 6 am and most days Angus would join him on site by 7 am. Every now and again another local tradesman would arrive to help. Of course Reg paid Angus a daily rate and made sure that he agreed prices with tradesmen in advance. He kept a meticulous record of all the hours Angus worked. He did not want anything to spoil their friendship. The two men worked well together. Sometimes Reg would learn from Angus's previous experience building his own home; at other times Reg would suggest methods he had used during his army career. Occasionally Angus had duties on his croft that he simply had to attend to but quite often Ryan would stop by when an extra pair of hands was needed.

Ryan was doing well in his new job and his relationship with Raj seemed to be growing ever stronger. She had now moved out of her digs in the village and had moved in with Ryan. During the school holidays she came to help Phyllis with the paperwork one day a week. The women had, by now, become really close and Phyllis looked forward to her company. The extra pair of hands was also useful and when the site started to fill on 5th April and hoards of children descended on the reception to choose some sweets, Raj was suitably qualified to take charge of the children, leaving Phyllis to complete the booking in forms with new arrivals.

Fortunately Donnie was also on hand, deterring Norman from taking any opportunity to sneak on site. Everyone was helping in one way or another meaning that the new house was progressing to plan.

The house was typical of the style in the highlands - a timber frame, with block work at the base, which would be rendered and covered with roughcast, made from Skye marble shingle, before being painted white. The lounge was to be upstairs with a huge window looking out across the bay and two more dormer windows in the upstairs dining room and bedroom. Even more light was introduced by three Velux windows in the roof. Reg's project plan was well thought out meaning that he could engage the necessary tradesmen to help out at the appropriate moments.

Annie and the children came for a week of the Easter holidays but sadly Reg had not had the opportunity to finish the play equipment. He would definitely make the time to have it ready for the summer. When they took the family to see the progress on the house so far, William wanted to stay with his granddad but it was not a safe place for a child so, under protest, he was taken away by Phyllis and encouraged to play with the other children on site.

Annie had every intention of taking Phyllis back to Stirling to choose all the new furniture that she had assumed her mother would want but Phyllis was adamant that she would use her existing furniture from Worcester that Ryan had put into store.

"Don't you want to choose modern, new furniture" Annie asked her Mum "The house won't look the same with the old things you've had for years."

Phyllis however had left that materiality behind. She had enjoyed her Christmas shopping trip but had to admit that she was no longer comfortable browsing busy department stores for the latest trends. Her pleasures now came more simply from her environment and the sheer beauty that was all around her. These things now meant more to her than money could buy. She was sure that if Henry were still here, he would also approve. Meg, Pat, Joyce, Hamish and all the other older, local people had taught her that real satisfaction can come from many things but seldom does a new car or new piece of furniture bring lasting contentment.

Once again the children enjoyed a holiday week of sheer delight. William was mud-splattered most of the time and Ellie played with the others along the shore. Both of them looked weathered and well, having benefitted from the many hours spent outdoors. When they returned home to their dad they all looked forward to their next visit in the summer holidays and seeing nanny and granddad's finished home, even though Reg kept telling them that he was not expecting completion until at least July.

Easter was largely good weather but in late April and May there were days when it was not possible to make much progress. In the first week of June, a tradesman arrived to put the roof on. Reg had decided that this element of the project required a specialist and it tied in nicely with Angus attending a show near Inveraray in which he had entered Archie, hoping to win a prize for the best one year old bull. Angus was quietly confident. Archie had grown a good set of horns, at least a foot long, straight but turning up slightly at the end. His coat was beautifully golden and his dossan or fringe was already covering his eyes, almost reaching his nose. He still had quite tufty ears and a clean, neat nose and was showing all the stocky features of a fine bull. Angus felt sure that Norman was aware what was happening when he saw Archie having a final wash and brush up outside the barn. He even thought that Norman was jealous judging by his mood the following day. This youngster would never steal his thunder!

Once the roof was on, progress was noticeable. The windows went in and an electrician spent several days placing the light switches, the sockets and the consumer unit in the specified places. Reg, determined to get the work finished, worked later into the evening but Phyllis gave him a strict 8pm deadline worried that, at his age, he might overstretch himself. Together with Angus, he installed the kitchen, the utility room, the main bathroom and their en-suite. Phyllis had of course taken some time out to choose the cupboards, the sanitary fittings and the tiles.

All the time that Reg had been so busy, Phyllis had coped admirably with running the site. She had welcomed many caravanners, a large group of ramblers with their tents and even more students attracted by Donnie's kayak business. Each season the number of visitors seemed to be growing as word of the site and its excellent facilities spread. Phyllis was also having an exceptional year with all her troughs and hanging baskets. With her new greenhouse she had been able to bring on her begonias and bedding plants in the warmth, only bringing them out when they were in their full glory. She spent every spare moment, not that she had many, in the greenhouse. What a wonderful present her husband had made for her.

They were really pleased when their old neighbours from Worcester, Annette and Keith, came, unannounced, to stay at Meg's. They shared a lovely evening with them catching up on all the old news and told them that they would be welcome to come and stay in the new house when it is finished.

"You've really got a lovely place here" said Keith.

"But if you don't mind me saying so Reg, you really do look tired" added Annette.

"Well its not many 68 year olds that take on a project like this" laughed Reg.

"I think that you'll need a good holiday when the house is finished" suggested Annette.

Reg simply smiled and shrugged. He couldn't think of anywhere else that he would want to go on holiday. Throughout their 40 years of marriage they had cruised the Caribbean, visited the pyramids, even been on safaris in Africa but nothing any longer held a candle to Scotland and he doubted that he would ever be enticed anywhere else. Their friends stayed well into the evening but when they saw that Reg had finally fallen asleep they realised that it was time to leave. Phyllis got their coats, thanked them for visiting and reiterated her invitation to their new home. After they had gone, she got a blanket from the cupboard and quietly placed it over Reg.

Seeing how tired Reg had become, Phyllis asked Ryan if he could spare the time to finish and erect the play equipment before the summer visitors came. At first Reg resisted. It was his project and one that he wanted to see to the end but he soon gave way. He insisted on spending time with Ryan explaining what needed to be done and choosing the exact spot on the site where each piece needed to be placed. With Donnie's help the younger men finished the work in just a couple of days. Ellie and William were arriving soon so it was agreed that the grandchildren would do the official opening.

Angus had enjoyed great success with Archie at the Inveraray show. He had impressed the judges and won first prize. He was given a large yellow rosette which totally complimented his colour. Several breeders had asked Angus whether he would sell him but Angus wasn't interested. He had his own plans for using Archie to service his cows in the future but he didn't let on to Norman, who was quite possessive when it came to the ladies. He did intend to offer

Archie's services out to other breeders for a price! As he was only just over a year, he could possibly already father offspring but Angus knew it would be better to leave it until he matured at about three or four years old.

When the grandchildren arrived they were naturally excited to be the first to use the play equipment. Reg took the time to watch them, feeling really proud as they obviously loved the tractor and the house. William now seemed far too occupied with this new attraction to follow his granddad everywhere - in fact it was hard for Annie to prise him away. Ellie nominated herself as warden of the play area, issuing instructions to all the other children. It was not difficult to see who she took after.

Regarding the stunning new house, Annie and Craig were thoroughly impressed with the progress that Reg and Angus had made. With only the tiles to put up and some internal painting to be done, Reg and Phyllis would soon be able to move in. Phyllis did go to Fort William with Annie simply to order the carpets that she needed for the bedrooms and choose a new rug to place on the wooden floor in the lounge. In the meantime, Ryan made the necessary arrangements for a removal firm to bring the furniture on 19th July by which time Reg had agreed that the house should be ready.

The busy site and the constant comings and goings of visitors made early July pass quickly and it was soon the day of the furniture delivery. Phyllis had forgotten how many boxes she had taped up but, predictably, Reg had meticulously recorded the contents on each box so he was able to tell the removal men exactly where to place each one. They had asked their friends and family to let them settle in before coming to a 'home warming' on 3rd August.

Elaine prepared a beautiful invitation for them.

*Phyllis and Reg*
*invite you to their 'home warming' at Taigh Bruadair*
*(next to Camus Caravan and Camping Site)*
*on 3rd August at 8pm*

Phyllis and Reg together had chosen the house name. They wanted to use a Gaelic name which complimented 'Camus' the Gaelic name of their site. Taigh Bruadair means Dream House which so aptly reflected how they had both come to feel.

It took them a while to organise their belongings, especially when they went upstairs to the lounge where they were often distracted by such fantastic views. By now the evenings were long and they would sit together, with a glass of wine or two, watching the sun go down behind the mountains way off in the distance. Life had certainly brought them a long way: from their application to be wardens of what initially seemed a remote, unloved caravan site to now be managing their own idyllic site; from arriving in unfamiliar territory to now being a treasured part of the community; from living in their small caravan to now enjoying such a wonderful new home; from preparing to spend their retirement following the same routine as many others to now enjoying their new life and embracing every challenge.

Phyllis looked across at Reg. The tiredness had lifted from his face and was replaced with a look of real contentment. He was spoilt for choice between the sight of the wondrous views before him and Maureen's painting of Fergal hanging proudly on the wall.

Phyllis too sat quietly with the treasured words of Donnie Munro, the former lead singer of Runrig, going round in her mind. She had first heard them on a DVD she had borrowed from Elaine.

*"Special places can be wherever you want them to be.*
*By being in them they root you and they tie you*
*And they give you a certain kind of strength".*

Phyllis now found that his beautiful choice of words was truly emblematic of how she had come to feel. Could they have been written with Camus in mind? From the start of their venture Camus had certainly been 'Calling'. At last it seemed that Camus had surely provided all the 'Answers'.

# ABOUT THE AUTHOR

When Jessie MacQuarrie retired from work, having been diagnosed with Multiple Sclerosis, she wrote her first novel 'Camus Calling'. Following many requests she has now written 'Camus Answers' the sequel, continuing with the much loved characters.

Fortunate to now own a mobility scooter Jessie has been able to continue her passion for the outdoors and particularly Scotland. Although she may not be able to climb mountains any longer she has grown to appreciate everything that this magical landscape offers.

Jessie has been inspired by the people she has met on her many caravan holidays along the West Coast. She has also learned a lot about the history and culture of the area. She vividly describes the colours she sees through the seasons and the wildlife encounters she has been privileged to experience.

Jessie has family history on the islands of Mull and Ulva. The novels subtly introduce the MacQuarrie clan to whom Jessie is related and refer to the sad days of the Highland

Clearances which have been passionately researched by her husband.

Throughout her travels Jessie has been touched by the welcoming nature and the kindness of local people which features strongly throughout both novels and has left an enduring legacy.

The storylines introduce humorous caravan capers; many are based on Jessie's own encounters. Both Camus Calling and Camus Answers will appeal to those who enjoy caravanning, those who love the Highlands and those who face the challenges of age or disability but refuse to give in!